Love Your Enemies

Love Your Enemies

NICOLA BARKER

faber and faber
LONDON · BOSTON

First published in 1993
by Faber and Faber Limited
3 Queen Square London WC1N 3AU

Phototypeset by Wilmaset Ltd, Wirral
Printed in Great Britain by Clays Ltd, St Ives plc

A CIP record for this book
is available from the British Library

ISBN 0–571–16769–1

2 4 6 8 10 9 7 5 3 1

Contents

For my sister, Tania

Layla's Nose Job

Layla Carter was just about as happy as it was possible for a sixteen-year-old North London girl to be who possessed a nose at least two centimetres longer than any nose among those of her contemporaries. As with all subjects of a sensitive nature, the length of Layla's nose was an issue of great topicality and contention. Common clichés such as 'Don't be nosy' or 'You're getting up my nose', even everyday phrases like 'Who knows?' – especially when uttered by an errant younger brother with a meaningful glance at the relevant part of Layla's physiognomy – would cause an atmosphere of hysterical teenage uproar in the Carters' semi-detached in the leafy suburbs of Winchmore Hill.

Layla sensed that the source of her problem was genetic, but neither of her parents, Rose and Larry Carter, possessed noses of any note. Her three siblings were blessed with lovely, truffling pink snouts with snub ends and tiny nostrils. They had nothing to complain about.

Her nose had always been big. On family occasions like Christmas or Easter when her grandparents and great aunts descended on the Carter household for a roast lunch and a glass of Safeways own-brand port, the family photo albums would be dragged out of the cabinet under the television and all tied by blood and name would pore over them and sigh.

No one sighed louder than Layla. Her odyssey of agony and self-consciousness began with her christening snaps and continued well after the visitors had gone home, the washing-up had been done and the living-room carpet hoovered.

As far as she could tell, her nose had always been disproportionate. She had often had recourse to see other people's christening photographs, and in none of them that she could remember had so many profile shots been taken to so much ill effect. Her nose emerged like a shark's fin from between the delicate folds of her fine, pearly-white shawl, and the sight of it cut into her stomach like a blade.

She struggled to remember a time when the size of her nose hadn't been a full-time preoccupation. As a young child in her first weeks at school, after a particularly violent spate of playground jousting – little boys shouting 'big nose' at her for a period in excess of fifteen minutes – her class teacher had bustled her, howling, into the staff-room and had dried her eyes, saying softly, 'When you grow older you'll study the Romans. They were the people who built all the best, long, straight roads in Britain, many, many years ago. Now just you guess what all of the Romans had in common? They all had fine aquiline noses. Long, straight, proud noses like yours. One day you'll learn to be proud of your nose too. You'll learn that all the best people have strong, bold, expressive faces and strong, proud, dignified noses.' She offered Layla a tissue and said, 'Now go on, blow.' Layla pushed her face forward and then felt a pang of intense misery as her nose poked a hole through the centre of the tissue; like a dog jumping through a paper hoop. Nothing could console her.

People are so cruel, children are so cruel. In the school playground as she grew older, worse humiliations were in store. Her nose became her central signifier. Whenever her best friend Marcy was deputized to approach a handsome young buck for whom Layla had developed a girlish passion, she would always see him turn to Marcy with a frown and say, 'Layla? Who's she?'

By way of explanation Marcy would invariably point her out as she stood skulking in the corner of the playground closest to the girls' toilets and say, 'That's her there. You know, the one with the big nose.'

Marcy always apologized for her indiscretions. She was a sympathetic girl, but she came from a big family where sensitivity and tact often had to be abandoned in the arena of attention-grabbing. She would say to Layla, 'I'd much rather have a big nose than no nose at all.'

Neither of them had ever seen anyone without a nose before, but as the years dragged by Layla regularly stood in front of her bedroom mirror with her hand covering this offending part of her face in an attempt to perceive herself, and her other features, without its overwhelming presence. The result was often quite gratifying. Whenever she tried moaning to her mother, Rose would say, 'Just be grateful for what you have got. You've got pretty blue eyes and lovely soft, brown, curly hair. You've got a good figure too. Be grateful. Try not to be so negative.' In return, Layla would grimace and shout, 'God! It's bad enough having a nose like Mount Everest – I'd hardly tolerate being fat as well. I have to make the best of myself, but that doesn't make things any better. In some ways that makes things worse. If I was truly ugly, what would I care if I had a big nose?'

She wished she could chop it off. When she was twelve, a short burst of appointments with the school therapist brought more light to this preoccupation. The therapist told Rose and Larry that Layla's regular association in her conscious and unconscious mind with chopping and removal implied a rather unusual and boyish adherence to what is commonly called the castration complex. He said, 'Layla wants to be a man. She wants to rival her father, Larry, for Rose's love and attention. Unfortunately she has no penis. This makes the penis a hate object. She wants to castrate Larry's penis because she is jealous of it. She feels guilty about her aggressive impulses towards Larry and so turns these feelings of violence on to herself. To Layla, her nose is a penis. Her hatred of her nose is symbolic of her hatred of her own sexuality. When she comes to terms with that, she'll be a happier and more complete person.'

After their appointment the Carters took Layla for a hamburger at the MacDonalds in Enfield's town centre as a treat. She sipped her milkshake and frowned. She said, 'What difference does all this make to me? Talking won't change the size of my nose, will it? Why does everyone have to pretend that my nose isn't the problem but that I am? It's as if everyone who wants to help me is determined to believe that my nose isn't all that big at all. But it is. It is!'

She had made her point. The family paid no heed to the therapist's recommendations. Except Larry, who took to locking the bedroom and the bathroom doors whenever he happened to undress; especially when shaving. He must have felt guilty about something.

By the time that she was fifteen, Layla knew everything conceivable about dealing with an outsize nose. She knew how to react when boys got on to the school bus in the afternoons and laughed at her and gesticulated, she knew how to comb and style her hair in a way that helped to accentuate her better features as opposed to her worse, she knew how to avoid having her photograph taken on family occasions (on holiday and at home), she knew how to spend hours every morning with a make-up brush and facial foundation, shading the sides of her nose and lightening its centre in a way she'd seen depicted in hundreds of teenage girls' magazines. Most of all she knew how to focus on this one, single thing. She made herself into a nose on legs.

She could not read a magazine without studying the nose of every model on its waxy, paper pages. If a model had a slightly larger nose than usual she would tear out the picture and put it into a scrapbook or stuff it in the drawer of her desk. At night she would list in her mind successful people who had big noses. She counted them like sheep in her pre-dream state; Chryssie Hynde, Margaret Thatcher, Barbra Streisand, Bette Midler, Dustin Hoffman, Rowan Atkinson, Cher. She thought about Cher quite a bit, because Cher had had her nose fixed.

In her dreams she visualized a scalpel, and its sharp edge touched her face like a kiss. It sliced her nose away so that her face felt light and radiant. But when she tried to bring her hand to her face to feel her new nose, her arms felt terribly heavy and could not be lifted. She used all her energy and willpower to attempt to lift them but they would not move. At this point she would awake from her dream and discover that she was actually trying to lift her arms, her real arms. In an instant she could then lift them to her face, and feel her face, and feel that everything was still the same. Even in her dreams, wish-fulfilment had its limits. Nothing ever went all the way.

Layla's problems were more than just cosmetic when she was fifteen. At this time Marcy began going out with her first serious boyfriend. Although they remained best friends this meant that Marcy grew less supportive towards Layla and increasingly preoccupied with her new relationship. She also became enthusiastic about the idea of Layla becoming involved in a relationship herself. Layla had very high standards. All the boys who supposedly found her attractive did so (she firmly believed, and with some grounds), because they were universally unattractive themselves.

But the pressure was on. Marcy visualized the 'double date' as the height of teenage sophistication and sociability. 'Imagine how much fun we could have if you and someone else could come out with me and Craig,' she'd say.

One warm summer Wednesday afternoon after school, Layla and Marcy went for a brisk stroll around the precinct in the town centre, looking at clothes, talking about teachers and drinking root beer. They ended up at Waitrose, where they bought a packet of Yum-Yum doughnut twists. Marcy suggested that they eat them on a bench in the park.

It was a set-up. Layla had barely taken the first bite of her doughnut when Craig turned up with one of his friends, Elvis. Her heart plummeted. After mumbling hello she walked a short distance to feed the rest of her Yum-Yum to a wayward duck. After a minute or so Marcy came over to her. She took her arm and said, 'Don't you like Elvis? Craig and I thought you'd get along.'

Layla baulked at this. She said, 'You thought we'd get along because we both have big noses, is that it?'

Marcy laughed nervously. 'Of course not. He's Jewish. Lots of Jewish men have big noses, it's natural.'

Layla forgot herself and wiped her sticky hands on her school dress. When she spoke again, her voice was dangerously calm. 'Of all the boys in the school you choose the one with the biggest nose to match me up with. You're supposed to be my best friend.'

'Lots of women think that Jewish men are very sexy, that their big noses are sexy,' Marcy interrupted.

Layla exploded, 'I hate big noses. I hate my nose. Why the hell should I want to go out with someone with an enormous nose?'

The two boys had turned to face them from their position by the

5

bench. Elvis looked flushed and irritated. Craig was laughing. He called over, 'You know what they say about men with big noses, don't you, Layla? They've got the biggest pricks.' He turned to Elvis. 'You'll vouch for that, won't you?'

Elvis was extremely angry. He said, 'You know what they say about girls with big noses, don't you, Layla? They say that they're very, very, very ugly, and that no one wants to go out with them.' He showed her one finger.

Her face went crimson. Marcy tried to defuse the situation. She rubbed Layla's arm apologetically. 'He's normally quite nice. I think he overheard us. He was upset, he didn't mean what he said.'

Layla pulled her arm away with great violence, the force of which pushed her a step backwards and sent the duck skittering off. 'Thanks a lot. Thanks for really humiliating me. I thought you were my friend. I suppose you and Craig had a real laugh planning this.'

Elvis had marched off in disgust, but Craig had made his way over to Marcy's side and put his arm protectively around her shoulders. 'Marcy was only trying to be nice. You make a mistake in thinking that everyone else is as interested in your stupid nose as you are. Elvis would've been a fool to want to go out with you, anyway. You're too self-obsessed.'

Layla strode over to the bench where she had left her school bag, and picked it up by its strap. Then she turned and said, 'Just because I have a big nose you all feel you've got the right to look down on me. I can just imagine Elvis and I going out on a date. Everyone who saw us would say, "Isn't it nice that two such strangely deformed people have found each other." I suppose it's like two dwarves going out together or two blind people, or two people with terrible speech impediments who could spit and stutter at each other over Wimpy milkshakes. Well, I want better than that. I'm more than just a big nose. I thought I was your best friend, Marcy, but in fact I'm just your big-nosed friend. That's all I am.'

Marcy said nothing as Layla sped away across the park.

That night when she got home Layla went straight to her bedroom. She locked the door and wouldn't come out. Rose left her a dinner-tray outside the door. She was concerned for Layla. The previous week she had seen a programme on teenage suicide. Layla was so volatile. Larry told her not to worry.

Layla sat alone and did a lot of thinking. She tried to analyse her world view. She tried to get outside herself and to see her situation from all angles. One central problem faced her: had other people made her self-conscious about her nose, or was she just vain, as Craig had implied? Had she created the problem for herself, or had society made her nose into a monster? Obviously her nose had always been in the centre of her face and it had always been big, but was that in itself enough to destroy her life?

She thought about Elvis and wondered how much consideration he gave to the size of his nose. But his was a Jewish nose. Hers was just a big nose. She knew that the size of Elvis's nose fitted into a larger scheme of things. It had a cultural space. It meant something. She thought, 'If you're Jewish and have a big nose it's like being Barbra Streisand or Mel Brooks. It means that you have a history, that you belong. The shape of my nose is just a mistake. My problem is stuck right bang in the centre of my face, and it has no wider implications than that. My problem is my nose. I didn't make the problem, the problem made me.'

It was so simple. It had to come off.

Late that evening she went downstairs into the living room and switched off the television. She stood in front of the screen – like a wonderful character from a film or a soap – and she announced firmly, 'Either I have a nose job or I kill myself. I can't go on like this any longer. I've heard that you can have one on the National Health. If you both love me you will help me.' She swayed gently as though she were about to swoon, then gathered herself up and strode from the room like Boadicea approaching her chariot: a woman with swords on her wheels.

Rose made an appointment with their local GP the following afternoon. Layla took an hour off school. She explained her problem to the GP and he agreed to book her in with a specialist.

7

Five months later Layla met the specialist. He was called Dr Chris Shaben and was a small, vivacious, balding man with a crooked face and yellowy teeth. Apparently he had a very beautiful wife. His surgery was on Harley Street and the gold plaque on his door said, 'Dr Chris Shaben, Plastic Surgeon' in a beautiful flowing script.

Layla sat in his office and discussed her nose at great length. For the first time ever she felt as though she was actually talking to someone who cared, someone who understood, and best of all, someone who could do something. It was as a dream to her. Entering his surgery had been like a scene of recognition in a book or a film; that moment when everything falls into place. It was an ecstatic moment. Layla was like a newborn child finding its mother's milky nipple for the first time.

It took a while to convince Dr Shaben that she was desperate and sincere. He said, 'Normally we only do plastic surgery treatments on the National Health if the problem involved is more than just cosmetic, but I'm willing to make an exception in this instance, Layla. Although you're young, you're very articulate and intelligent. I realize that your concerns go deeper than mere vanity.'

Layla nodded. She said slowly, 'For a while I tried to make myself believe that *I* had made the size of my nose into an issue, that the problem was to do with me, on the inside, not the out. My parents encouraged this line of thought, although my Mum has always been supportive, and my analysis did the same thing. But now I know that the problem is on the outside too. People judge one another visually; I should know, I do it myself. I want to be normal. I want to stop being on the outside, the periphery.'

Dr Shaben nodded and smiled at Layla. His bald head and short stature made him look like a tiny, benign, laughing Buddah as he sat hunched and serene in his big, leather, office chair.

Before the operation Layla abandoned her GCSE course work and concentrated instead on the leaflets, diagrams and information surrounding the surgery that she was about to undertake. She read how modern technology now meant that some nose operations could be undertaken entirely through the nostrils without any recourse to external incisions and unsightly scarring. The nose was chiefly made up out of bone and gristle, but was also extremely sensitive because of the large number of nerve endings at its tip. She tested this theory by smacking her nose with a pencil and then smacking other parts of her face like her cheeks and eyebrows. The nose was much more delicate. After the operation, a certain amount of swelling and bruising was to be expected.

Four days after her sixteenth birthday Layla awoke in a large and unfamiliar room. Her duvet was tightly stretched across her chest and felt unusually harsh and full of static. She was dopey. Her throat felt weird and dry. Her nose was numb but ached. She thought for an instant that she was dreaming her nose dream, that she wanted to put her hands to her face but her hands were restricted, yet after a few minutes she realized that she was in a strange bed in a strange environment. It was no dream, but her arms were restricted by the tightness of her sheets and blankets. She wriggled her body gently to create some room and worked her hands free. She placed them on her face. Her nose hurt. Her hands touched soft, filmy bandage and Band-Aid. It was done.

For the next five days her head felt light. Dr Shaben said that it was simply psychological, but she felt the lightness of a person who once had long hair and then cut it short, the roomy strangeness of someone who has had their arm broken and set in plaster and then has the plaster removed so that their arm floats up into the air because it feels so odd and weightless and light.

At first her face looked swollen and ugly. In hospital she wore no make-up and was blue with bruises. But she could see the difference. In the mirror her nose looked further away. Dr Shaben was pleased for her. He was well satisfied.

Throughout her stay in hospital, Rose had been in to see her every day. Larry preferred to stay away. Before she had gone in on her first night he had said to her, 'Remember how when you were small I would sit you on my knee and bounce you up and down and call you my little elephant girl? You always laughed and giggled. It's not like that any more. Now you've grown up into someone I don't recognize. I can't approve of what you are doing. God made you as you are. That should be enough.'

This came as a great shock to Layla. She had completely forgotten Larry's pet name for her. When she heard him say it again it was like a blow to her face, a blow to her nose, making it ache, making her numb. It was a kind of violent anaesthetic.

She was being pulled in so many directions. Everyone had a different opinion as to the whys and wherefores. Rose simply said, 'Do whatever will make you happy.'

After five days she came home. Although she was still slightly bruised, the mirror was her friend. Her three brothers greeted her at the front door with euphoric whoopings. Larry sat in the living room, watching the cricket. He turned after a minute or so and saw her, standing nervously by the door, her hands touching the bookcase for support. First he smiled, then he laughed, 'Five days away, all that money spent, and look at you. No difference! You look no different.' He laughed on long after she had left the room, but when he'd finished his stomach felt bitter.

Later Marcy visited. She smiled widely and hugged Layla like a real friend. Then she looked closely at her nose and said, 'Maybe your nose looks slightly different, but to me you are still the same old Layla. In my mind's eye you are exactly the same person. Nothing has changed.' She thought that she was saying the right thing.

Layla sat alone upstairs in her room, staring into the mirror. She felt sure that she looked different. She felt sure that she was now a different person, inside. But the worry now consumed her that other people would not be able to see how different she looked. It felt like a conspiracy. She thought, 'Maybe I've become the ugly person I was outside, inside. Perhaps that can never be changed.' She felt like Pinocchio.

That night she had a dream. In her dream she was a tiny little elephant, but she was without a trunk. She had four legs and thick grey skin, big flapping ears and a thin end-tassled tail. But she had no nose. Because she had no nose she couldn't pick things up – to eat, to wash, to have fun – all these things were now impossible. It was like being without arms. She kept asking for help. Her mother smiled and stroked her, but everyone else just laughed and pointed.

She slept late. When she awoke she felt battered and exhausted. When she looked into the mirror, her old face looked back at her. Nothing had changed. She felt utterly helpless. Her mind rambled and a thousand different images moved through the space behind her eyes. Her head was full of colour. She saw different people too, pointing their fingers, wiping her nose, holding her arm, bouncing her up and down on their knee, up and down, up and down.

In the kitchen she looked for a small knife to cut the top off her boiled egg. Instead she found that she had a chopping knife in her hand and it was as long as her arm. She cut the egg in half and its yolk hit the wall. She placed the blade near to her nose and felt tempted to move it closer. She stopped. For hours she remained stationary.

Larry had forgotten his sandwiches. He drove home in his lunch hour and let himself into the quiet house. He went upstairs for a quick pee. For once he neglected to shut and lock the door. He whistled contentedly.

Downstairs in the kitchen Layla's mind started to turn again. She considered her options.

A Necessary Truth

Sammy Jo burped the baby and then lay her down on her pink, rubber changing mat and began to unpin her nappy. The baby puffed a gentle tongueful of spew out of her tiny mouth and down the side of her chin. Sammy Jo undid the nappy and then, almost without thought, used one of its Terry corners to mop up the sick. She lifted the baby's head up, gently supporting its weight in her free hand, to make sure that her mouth was now empty. She didn't want her to choke accidentally.

The baby was called Charlie, short for Charlotte. She was four months old. Sammy Jo tossed the nappy into the (thankfully close) washing basket and carefully laid Charlie's head down again. She picked up a clean nappy and formed it into the requisite shape. The baby wheezed quietly.

Sammy Jo stared out of the window for a moment and caught sight of her husband Jason hanging out some nappies on the line. She rolled her tongue around the long nappy pin with its baby pink tip which she had stuck in the corner of her mouth – like a metal cigarette – while she felt around sightlessly on the table for some baby-wipes and talc.

The telephone rang. She grimaced to herself, let go of the tin of talc and then reached over to pick it up. Charlie screwed up her face at the sudden sharpness of the ringing – she couldn't decide whether to cry or not – and then relaxed again when it stopped. Sammy Jo carried on staring out of the window. 'Yes?'

She never said anything but 'yes' when she answered the telephone. Her biggest mistake in the past had been repeating her name and number on answering. She now knew that if you say your name and number some strange people copy this information down when they hear a woman's voice. Then they telephone you again and again and turn your life into a living hell.

Sammy Jo's telephone number was ex-directory. All the people who now had her number were people that she definitely trusted; a mere handful. This system had hitherto proved virtually foolproof.

A voice said, 'What can we be sure of in our life? What two things can we infer – almost immediately – without needing to resort to empirical information?'

Sammy Jo's eyes snapped away from the window and focused, somewhat pointlessly, on the telephone receiver in her hand. The voice continued, 'By empirical I mean "information derived from experience". Does all this sound rather confusing? Don't let it confuse you. I've already confused myself. Bringing in the notion of empirical experience – Locke, Hume, remember those names – has confused things already. Let's start again.'

Sammy Jo slammed down the receiver. She stood up and searched around for some paper and a pen. She found a thick telephone pad with slightly sticky adhesive edges which she had been given (months before) by her local independent pizza restaurant and take-away. Each piece of paper was shaped like a red and yellow pizza, intermittently round, with the address and telephone number of the restaurant in small print at the top.

She placed the pad on the table in between the telephone and the baby and began to write: *Man, Thirty/forty, deep but weak voice – muffled? Breathy.*

She paused and thought for a moment and then wrote: *Rubbish, not offensive.* She crossed out the word *offensive* and then wrote *sexual* instead. She bit her lip. The telephone rang again. She stared out of the window towards Jason (who still seemed rather preoccupied) and then slowly, hesitantly, picked up the receiver. A voice said, 'Hi! Sammy Jo?' Sammy Jo breathed a sigh of relief and relaxed visibly. She smiled. 'Hello. Yes?'

'Hi Sammy, it's Lucy here, Lucy Cosbie. How are things?'

Sammy Jo pinched the receiver between her shoulder and her ear while using her two free hands to grab a tissue and wipe Charlie's bottom. Charlie let out a small whimper, but Lucy Cosbie heard it. 'Is that Charlie there?'

Sammy Jo grinned. 'Yeah. I'm changing her. I haven't seen you for a couple of months, Lucy. You must pop around when you're free. Jason mentioned you only the other day . . .'

Lucy's laughter echoed down the telephone line. 'Wow! I must be making progress if Jason's asking about me!'

Sammy Jo clucked her tongue and picked up the talc. 'Don't be stupid. In a way I think he kind of misses you.'

Lucy stopped laughing and said, 'Well, this is just a semi-professional informal call. I wanted to make sure that things are fine, that everything is going well, you know . . .'

Sammy Jo finished talcing the baby's bottom and put the talc bottle down on the table. She stared guiltily at the pizza pad in front of her and touched what she had written on the pad with her index finger. She then said, 'Honestly, Lucy, everything's great. I already have my midwife coming around every other week to check up on Charlie's progress. She's doing just fine. I think enough of the council's resources have been spent on me already without you worrying too . . .'

Lucy was sensitive to Sammy Jo's tone. She said lightly, 'Sammy Jo, relax. I'm not checking up on you. I know how sensitive young mums can be. I'm honestly not intruding, just interested.'

Sammy Jo interrupted, breathless with embarrassment. 'Lucy, I'm sorry. I didn't mean it to sound like that, honestly. I'm just a bit uptight today. You're more than welcome here any time. In fact, why don't we make a date for a visit right now? How about Thursday afternoon?'

Sammy Jo could hear the busy noises of an office and a typewriter behind Lucy's voice. Lucy said, 'Hey! I'm quite a busy person, Sammy Jo. I'm afraid Thursday's a bit tight for me. I tell you what, why don't I ring in a couple of weeks' time and we can make an evening arrangement? Something purely social. That way the neighbours can't possibly have anything to gossip about, especially if I arrive on your doorstep after six-thirty with a bottle of wine. How about it? Purely informal. I'm desperate to see that gorgeous baby again.'

Sammy Jo smiled. 'I don't care what anyone thinks, Lucy. I'd love to see you, any time of day. Telephone soon, OK?'

15

They exchanged their farewells.

Sammy Jo put down her receiver and reached out to pick up Charlie's legs, lifted them up a few inches and slid the nappy underneath her whitely talced bottom. Before she could complete her nappy-tying, Jason had strolled into the room with the bag of remaining clothes pegs tucked under his arm. He said, 'Did I hear the telephone ring?'

Sammy Jo nodded. 'Yes. It was Lucy Cosbie.'

He raised his eyebrows, rather cynically. 'Checking up? I didn't think you were her department any more.'

Sammy Jo smiled. 'I'm not. Just a social call, that's all.' She pushed the nappy pin into Charlie's nappy and, picking her up, said, 'Look, Jason, Charlie's left you a little present in the washing basket.'

Jason looked down at the basket and let out a howl of horror. 'Bloody hell! You'd think we had a production line of babies in here, not just one, with the amount of waste she produces. I'm sure that when she eventually gets around to speaking, her first coherent words will be "More washing, Daddy."'

Sammy Jo was looking around for one of Charlie's clean romper suits. Before she could say anything Jason said, 'In the pile on the sofa. Would you mind putting on some rubber knickers this time so it doesn't get soaked in twenty seconds?'

She winked. 'Oh, Jason, you never said you liked me in rubber before!'

He smiled and shook his head. 'I know that I agreed to take responsibility for the washing of nappies and stuff if we had a baby, Sammy Jo, but tomorrow I have a lot of work on so I might just pop out and buy a packet or two of disposables, all right? Just for one day.'

Sammy Jo shrugged, unmoved, 'I don't care, Jason, go ahead. You're the one who's so bothered about the environmental angle concerning disposables, not me. Buy them if you want to, feel free.'

Jason picked up his jacket, which was slung over the back of the sofa. He said, 'I'll pop out now. Do you want anything else?'

Sammy Jo smiled obsequiously. 'I'll write you a list.'

She looked around her and then saw the pizza pad on the table.

Jason was watching her as he pulled his jacket on. She saw the few words that she had scribbled on to the top of the pad and, trying not to frown, ripped the page away and screwed it up in her hand. Jason said, 'What's that? Beginning of your thesis?'

She grimaced. 'Very funny. Actually it was a trial shopping list, but I've now thought of several items extra, including five years' subscription to *Parenting* magazine.'

She wrote down a couple of things and then handed him the piece of paper. He took it and perused it for a second. 'For a frightening moment there I thought you were serious.'

She shrugged, 'You know me, Jason, happy with sterilizing liquid and rosehip syrup. I don't need anything else in my life.'

He raised his eyebrows in disbelief, chucked Charlie gently under her chin and said, 'I'll only be gone ten minutes or so, enjoy yourself.' Sammy Jo smiled.

When he had gone, she found a pair of rubber knickers, put them over Charlie's nappy and then manoeuvred the baby's tiny body into a yellow lambswool romper suit. She pulled a small, soft blanket from her cot by the window and wrapped her up in it, then lay her down inside the cot. Charlie squawked her disapproval as soon as Sammy Jo set her down. Sammy Jo steeled herself to ignore these noises and strolled into the kitchen to make a mug of tea. As she switched the kettle on the telephone started ringing. She paused for a moment and then went to answer it.

'Yes?'

A voice said, 'Forget all that crap about empirical information. I don't want to alarm you with big words before you've even got a grip on the basic ideas.'

Sammy Jo bit her lip, and then said violently, 'What makes you think that I don't understand what that word means? What the hell makes you presume that?'

Her heart sank. She hadn't intended to participate in this conversation at all. She knew that participation was half of the trouble with anonymous callers. It meant that you were condoning the act. Implicitly. She felt ashamed and stupid and thought, 'After all I've

17

been through, I'm still a silly, stupid novice. I haven't learned anything. I don't deserve people's help and advice.'

The voice continued, 'Let's go back to what I said first, Sammy Jo. That question about two things in life that we can be sure of. Two basic things.'

Sammy Jo's heart plummeted. She thought, 'My God, he knows my name. Did I say my name when I answered this time? Why did I answer him in the first place?'

She said, 'I guess I can be sure that you are telephoning me, irritating me, involving yourself in my life when all I really wish is that you were dead in a room somewhere or dying of a terrible disease, or at the very least in some fundamental physical discomfort.'

The voice cackled, 'Well done! That's part of the answer, Sammy Jo, very well done. To put it simply, the two things that we can really be sure of in life are (a) that we exist. We can be sure of ourselves. Are you in any doubt that you exist, Sammy Jo, any doubt at all?'

Sammy Jo sighed. 'The only thing I don't doubt is that you are a pain in the fanny. That's all.'

The voice paused for a moment and then said, 'I get your point. We know that we exist because we can feel pain. Our bodies feel pain. I can be sure of two things, to quote Russell: "We are acquainted with our sense-data and, probably, with ourselves. These we know to exist." Sense-data is a silly technical word which I'll explain to you later.'

Sammy Jo was biting her nails and looking around for the pen she'd used earlier to write her shopping list. To pass the time she said, 'Go away. I don't want to talk to you.'

The voice said, 'Imagine yourself in any situation, any situation at all. It doesn't matter what you imagine yourself doing.'

He paused. 'I knew it would come to this, he's going to talk dirty. I knew it,' Sammy Jo thought instantaneously. She felt familiar feelings of outraged passivity seeping into her chest. 'Go on, say it, you dirty bastard. Don't pretend that this is about anything else,' she said.

But the voice continued, 'No matter what you think, do or imagine,

18

the only constant element is you. You can't get away from yourself. You can imagine that the world is a figment of your imagination, that the sky is yellow but just seems blue, that your body doesn't really exist and that you are just imagining that it does, that you are in fact asleep and dreaming and not awake at all. Close your eyes.'

Automatically Sammy Jo closed her eyes and quickly opened them again. She hung up. The phone rang immediately. She let it ring about ten times until the repetitive noise it made began to upset Charlie and she began to splutter and howl. Sammy Jo felt guilty about letting it upset her and also couldn't help thinking that perhaps it was someone else. Eventually she picked it up. 'Yes?'

The voice continued, 'If you close your eyes it's possible to reject almost everything that seems predictable in everyday life.'

She sighed and then said bitterly, 'I can't deny the fact that you exist, though, can I? You exist, don't you?'

The voice was urgent and persuasive. 'No way. Think about it. Nothing exterior to your mind and your thought is necessary. Don't be confused by my use of the word "necessary" here. I used it in its philosophical context. By it I mean a Necessary Truth, something that cannot be denied. For all you know my voice could be just a figment of your imagination.'

Sammy Jo laughed, a guttural, cynical laugh. 'Oh, so now you're going to tell me that this telephone call, this infuriating interruption in my life, is my own fault. Is that it?'

'Could be.'

Sammy Jo sighed loudly. 'Well, if I made you up, how come you won't go away?'

There was a short silence. During this silence Sammy Jo picked up her pen and wrote the words NECESSARY TRUTH on the pizza pad in large capitals. The voice then said, 'Try and remember this phrase: I Think Therefore I Am. In Latin it goes *Cogito Ergo Sum*. I think is "*cogito*", c-o-g-i-t-o. Therefore is *ergo*, e-r-g-o. I am is *sum*, s-u-m. Got that?'

Sammy Jo finished writing down the last letter, then slammed her pen down on the table. 'What on earth makes you think I give a damn? You're boring me. Go and bore someone else.'

The voice said calmly, 'I want you to read something by a guy called Descartes tonight. He was the founder of modern philosophy – circa 1600. He invented something called "The Method of Systematic Doubt". If you can get hold of his *Meditations* I'd recommend the first chapter. It's only short.'

Sammy Jo said quickly, 'Forget it. I'll be much too busy this evening committing sodomy with my household pet and watching *Emmerdale Farm*.'

This time he rang off.

She picked up her pen again and wrote down the name Descartes (although she spelled it Deycart), then threw the pen down, tore off the top page of the pad, crumpled it up and threw it at the paper bin in the corner of the room. The paper missed the bin and hit the wall. She got up and went into the kitchen to finish making her cup of tea. While she was pouring in the milk Jason returned carrying a couple of bags of Pampers. He pinched her arm, 'Tea! Yes please!' She grimaced and bent down to get out another cup.

That night when they were both lying in bed waiting to go to sleep and listening out for Charlie's whimpers from her cot nearby, Sammy Jo took hold of Jason's arm and said, 'Jason, have you ever heard of Descartes?'

Jason yawned and turned over on to his back, 'I don't know, Sammy Jo. I have some vague ideas about him. Probably read him at college at some point. Why?'

Sammy Jo shrugged. 'Is it rude?'

Jason laughed. 'Not so far as I know. He was French, but that doesn't necessarily mean that he was a kinky writer.'

Sammy Jo sighed. 'Oh.'

Jason paused for a moment, then said, 'Sammy Jo, I didn't mean to be off-putting. If you're interested I might have a book on ancient philosophy downstairs that features him, but I can't be sure.'

Sammy Jo smiled. 'I don't think so, Jason. Apparently Descartes was the founder of modern philosophical thought.'

Jason opened his eyes and stared at her in the dark.

*

The following afternoon Sammy Jo had just returned from taking Charlie out for a walk in her pram and was taking off her coat and combing a hand through her rather windswept short, red hair, when the telephone started ringing. She picked Charlie up and went to answer it. It was the man again. She pulled the telephone over towards the sofa and sat down, balancing Charlie on her knees, supporting her with one hand. The man said, 'Hello, Sammy Jo. I suppose it would be optimistic of me to expect you to have read that chunk of Descartes' *Meditations* that I recommended to you last night? The first chapter, remember?'

Sammy Jo snorted. 'Why don't you just sod off?'

The man continued, 'After I rang off yesterday it occurred to me that I hadn't been particularly encouraging towards you, and that was very wrong of me. I think you did extremely well, all things considered. You are obviously an intelligent woman. I think you just need stretching.'

Sammy Jo shook her head, 'No, I don't need stretching. The only person who needs stretching around here is you, and by that I mean stretching on the rack. Ancient forms of torture. I like that idea.'

The man said quietly, 'Try not to be so combative, Sammy Jo. Let's just get back to Descartes and his Method of Systematic Doubt.'

Sammy Jo hung up. As she tucked Charlie up in her cot a good fifty seconds or so later, the telephone started to ring again. Sammy Jo finished arranging Charlie's covers and then, grabbing hold of her pizza pad and pen, went to answer it.

'Yes?'

The man said, 'Do you understand the word "scepticism", Sammy Jo? Try and give me a working definition.'

Sammy Jo was writing on her pad in untidy capitals. She wrote: I WILL NOT GIVE IN. I CANNOT GIVE IN. I SHALL NOT GIVE IN. I MUST TAKE POSITIVE ACTION . . . TELEPHONE JASON? TELEPHONE LUCY COSBIE? WHISTLE DOWN THE TELEPHONE?

The voice said, somewhat more harshly, 'Sammy Jo? Do you understand the meaning of the word scepticism?'

Sammy Jo threw down her pen and ripped the top page away

from her pad. She shouted, 'Of course I do. Don't patronize me. Of course I do.'

'Well, give me a working definition, then.'

'Why should I? Why?'

He sighed, 'Just to prove that you know.'

She laughed. 'I don't need to prove anything to you.'

'Well, prove it to yourself then.'

Sammy Jo hesitated for a moment, then picked up her pen again. She said quietly, 'All right then, I don't really understand what it means, properly. Tell me and I'll write it down.'

That night during dinner Sammy Jo asked Jason if he could get her a proper lined writing pad from work and a couple of spare biros. Jason was cutting up his fish fingers with one eye on the television, watching *Wogan*. Wogan was interviewing Candice Bergen. Jason put a mouthful of the battered fish into his mouth and chewed thoughtfully without replying. Sammy Jo glared at him. 'Jason, do you mind paying me some attention? I'm talking to you!'

He turned towards her. 'Something about paper and pens, right?'

She nodded. 'Would you get me some from work? They supply you free don't they?'

He frowned. 'What do you want them for?'

Sammy Jo turned her eyes towards the television screen and focused on Wogan's tie. 'Nothing in particular. Telephone messages, addresses, sometimes on daytime television they have interesting babycare tips and recipes and stuff. They'd just come in handy.'

Jason carried on eating, 'OK, I'll try and remember.'

The following day Sammy Jo left the house at eleven o'clock with Charlie tucked up in her pram, and went out shopping. She collected Charlie's child benefit money from the post office, then caught a bus into the centre of Milton Keynes. In her pocket was a piece of the pizza pad with the address of a bookshop scribbled on it. She found the bookshop and pushed her way clumsily inside. The

22

short, dark man standing behind his desk in the shop came forward to help her. He said, 'These places aren't designed with prams in mind.'

Sammy Jo smiled. 'Next time I'll remember that and leave the baby on the bus.'

He grinned. 'I didn't mean any offence. Leave the pram here by the till and I'll keep an eye on the baby while you browse.'

Sammy Jo let go of the pram and strolled around the shop. After several minutes she returned to the assistant and said, 'If I keep an eye on the baby, would you mind finding copies of these books for me?'

She handed him her piece of paper which he took from her and perused. He smiled – 'No problem' – and quickly located the volumes in question. She held the three thin books in her hands and looked guiltily at the prices. The assistant noticed her concern. He said, 'Specialist books are expensive on the whole, but I think you'll find that those are quite reasonable. Russell was a bit of a popularist – excluding his works on mathematical logic, of course – so his more general works are very reasonably priced. The Descartes is a fraction more expensive, but the Sartre isn't too bad. That's fiction though, *The Age of Reason*, it's a great book.'

Sammy Jo smiled at the assistant. He seemed enthusiastic and well read. She said, 'One day I hope to be as well informed as you are. Which book do you think I should read first?'

He shrugged. 'It depends on what you're after. If I were you I'd read *The Age of Reason* first. It's good to introduce yourself to ideas in an informal sort of way. Then the ideas just pop into your head and it's no strain to pick them up.'

Sammy Jo looked at the synopsis on the back of the Penguin paperback. 'It looks a bit heavy going.'

The assistant smiled sympathetically. 'You haven't bought it yet. You could always change your mind.'

Sammy Jo looked at him quizzically. 'Do you think I should?'

He chuckled, 'I'm playing the devil's advocate. The story is about free will, about a man's search for personal freedom. You should use your free will to decide whether you really want to buy it or not. If you choose to buy it then you will have made a commitment to the book. In fact you will have involved yourself in the book's fundamental dilemmas.'

His face glowed as he explained this to her. His green eyes shone and he seemed excited. Sammy Jo handed him the three books and said, 'All right, I'll have them. I'll read the . . .' she paused. 'Why are all these names so hard to pronounce?'

He took the books and put them into a bag. 'Say the word "start".'

Sammy Jo repeated after him, 'Start.'

'Then take out the first letter t so it's "sart".'

She copied him: 'Sart.'

'Then say the word "rough".'

She smiled. 'Rough.'

'But forget about the "ugh" part and just say "ro". Then altogether it's "Sartre". Obviously that's the simple English pronunciation, but people will know who you mean.'

Sammy Jo said the name out loud to him a few times and then handed him some of her child benefit money. She said, 'I'm going to start the Sartre on the bus home. I hope I enjoy it.'

He finished wrapping up her books and handed them over to her. 'That's entirely up to you.'

She grinned. 'That's a joke, right?'

When Sammy Jo got home she changed and fed the baby and then made herself a sandwich and sat down on the sofa to start Chapter Two of *The Age of Reason*. Her main thoughts about its central character, Mathieu, were that she was glad that he wasn't looking after her baby. He didn't seem responsible enough. When the telephone rang she told the man on the line these thoughts. She said, 'Ideas are all right, but ideas can't guide your life, it isn't practical or realistic.'

He laughed. 'So what do you think should be man's main motivation? The acquisition of food? Making cups of tea?'

She raised her eyebrows – fully cognizant of his cynicism – and stared out of the window. 'I wasn't saying that. I'm not quite so stupid. All I mean is that people can't afford to be so self-indulgent, so luxurious. You have to get on with things. My life would be in a fine mess if I suddenly decided that I wanted to be free, that I couldn't be bothered to look after my young baby any more because she gets in the way of my freedom and independence.'

The man sounded irritated. 'No, you're trivializing the issue. You decided to have the baby, you made that decision freely many months ago. You could have aborted the child had you felt otherwise. The character Mathieu isn't entirely unhindered in his decisions about whether he wants Marcelle's baby . . . that's silly, what I mean to say is that obviously he doesn't want a baby but he has other considerations to take into account; Marcelle's feelings, money, the illegality of abortions . . .'

Sammy Jo sighed, 'Men are bastards. Really it's her problem. He just worries about it to make himself feel good. He's a shit.'

He interrupted her. 'The character doesn't matter, Sammy Jo. It's his thoughts and actions that are our concern, not whether you happen to like him or not.'

Sammy Jo snorted. 'If I don't like the character how can I read and enjoy the book?'

His voice was sharp. 'That's stupid. Behave rationally. Since when do you have to like a character in order to be able to understand and sympathize with his dilemmas? You can't go through life saying, ''Oh, she doesn't sound very nice so I'm not interested in her.'' That's ridiculous. Those sorts of comments are unworthy of you. You should think beyond your own standpoint. If you can't do that, then a whole dimension is lost to you. Have you got a proper pad of paper now?'

Sammy Jo shrugged and didn't answer, like a petulant schoolgirl. The voice said, 'Sammy Jo, answer me.'

She hung up and stared at the telephone for several seconds, waiting for it to ring. It didn't. She stared at it for a full five minutes, then began to feel stupid. She walked over to Charlie, who was sleeping in her crib, warm and cosy, smelling of milk. Out in the garden a small grey cat was scratching its claws on the thin trunk of a small apple tree. She felt frustrated. She thought, 'What right does he have to manipulate me like this? He's imposing on me. He's a bully. It's wrong for strangers to interfere like this, to impose like

25

this, to telephone you when they want, to build up a relationship that depends solely on their goodwill . . .'

She scratched her head and said musingly to Charlie's tiny body, which, disguised by layers of soft blankets, just rose and fell with the repetitive lull of sleepy breathing, 'Charlie, people are strange. This man is strange. I suppose I should tell Jason really, but I know he'll just get upset. I could telephone Lucy Cosbie . . . but do I really need to? This situation is quite different from before, altogether different. No one is threatening me. I don't know.'

She went and sat down on the sofa and picked up her book again. She read until five and then went into the kitchen and started to prepare dinner. Jason came in while she was frying some courgettes and cutting mushrooms. He pecked her on the cheek and said, 'Do I guess from this that Charlie will be enjoying ratatouille-flavoured milk this evening?'

She smiled broadly. 'You're welcome to enjoy ratatouille-flavoured milk yourself this evening if you prefer, so long as there's enough to go around. I don't know how well garlic and tomatoes translate into a calcium drink, though.'

He shook his head. 'I think I'll skip that one, if you don't mind, Sammy Jo.'

The telephone rang. Jason immediately moved away from her as though to go and answer it. Sammy Jo grabbed hold of his arm and said hurriedly, 'Jason, I know who that is. It's for me. My mother said she'd ring this evening.' She pushed past him as she spoke. 'I'll get it. Stir the vegetables, all right?'

He nodded. She picked up the telephone. 'Hi, Mum. Jason's home now so I can't really talk for long.'

The man said, 'I want you to think about this question very carefully, Sammy Jo. Write it down.'

Sammy Jo picked up a pen and copied down his question with great care on the pizza pad, which was now greatly diminished in size. Then they both said goodbye.

As she put down the telephone receiver she caught sight of her three new books slung carelessly on to the sofa, *The Age of Reason* open face downwards towards the middle of the text, like a ballerina clumsily doing the splits and unable to rise from that position. Quickly she picked them up and walked over to Charlie's cot. Picking Charlie up she slid the books under the cot's small mattress, then carried Charlie into the kitchen. Jason was stirring the courgettes and mushrooms around in the frying pan, staring at the wall in front of him in a tired, unfocused way. He seemed ill-at-ease. Sammy Jo offered Charlie's sleepy body to him and said, 'Give me the wooden spoon in exchange for the baby. You can change her if you like.'

He smiled. 'What into? A well trained corgi?'

She frowned. 'Don't avoid the inevitable, Jason, she feels pretty wet to me.'

He sighed and took hold of Charlie's tiny body, then carried her into the sitting room. Sammy Jo opened a tin of tomatoes while he lay the baby down on her changing mat and searched around for one of the remaining disposable nappies. He said loudly, so Sammy Jo could hear him above the noise of the frying pan, 'How's your mother? You didn't chat for long.'

Sammy Jo added the tomatoes to the rest of the vegetables in the pan, then remembered she had forgotten to start with a chopped onion. She cursed under her breath, then said hastily, 'She's fine. She's a bit busy actually. I think she had plans to go out tonight.' Jason took off Charlie's dirty nappy and said, 'I'm so glad I don't have any washing to do this evening. I'm knackered. There again, it still makes my skin crawl to imagine what I'm doing to the environment with just one day's usage of these things.'

He turned Charlie over and cleaned her bottom with some tissues. Sammy Jo cleared her throat and appeared in the doorway. 'Did you get that paper for me, Jason?'

He nodded. 'Yeah. It's in my case, by the door.'

He lay one of the nappies out on the table and lifted up Charlie's legs so as to slide it under her bottom. As he performed this manoeuvre he stuck out one of his elbows and accidentally knocked the telephone with it. The telephone was balanced on the edge of the table and threatened to fall off. Quickly grabbing hold of it and pushing it a couple of inches away from the edge, he focused on the pad covered in small, neat print. He took hold of it with his free hand and perused it, initially with uninterest and then with some surprise. On the pad Sammy Jo had written: 'ARE GOOD AND EVIL OF IMPORTANCE TO THE UNIVERSE OR JUST TO MAN?' BERTRAND RUSSELL. THINK ABOUT THIS. He moved the pad closer to his face in order to reread these words. He frowned, put the pad down again and completed Charlie's nappy.

Sammy Jo strolled into the room clutching her new pad as Jason finished putting on Charlie's rubber knickers. She walked over and switched on the television, saying, 'Dinner shouldn't be long now. Pass her over, will you? I need to feed her.'

He picked up Charlie.

'Sammy Jo?'

'Yep?'

'This may sound rather stupid, but I couldn't help noticing what you have written down on the pad by the phone.'

She looked up guiltily and played for time. 'I can't remember writing anything. It can't have been important . . .' She put out her arms for Charlie. 'Pass her over please.'

He handed the baby over and watched dispassionately as Sammy Jo began breast-feeding. He said, 'Have you been watching the Open University while I'm out at work?'

Sammy Jo shrugged. 'I might have caught a programme at some point, Jason. I can't really remember. I don't just sit around all day watching television, you know. Looking after a young baby isn't just fun and games.'

He shook his head, bewildered. 'I wasn't suggesting that, Sammy Jo, not at all. Anyway, you wanted the baby, it was a decision you made freely, you were hardly under any pressure.'

Sammy Jo frowned. 'Freedom's not really like that, Jason. I've been giving it some thought lately. The way I see it, freedom is like a train journey. When you get on the train, everyone assures you that you are free to climb off whenever you choose, but as with all train journeys there doesn't seem much point getting off at most of the stations. They just aren't appropriate to your life. A lot of things dictate as to when and where you get off the train. It isn't just a random decision. The past propels you forward, and all your future decisions have already been made well in advance, dictated by age, class, sex . . . anyway, your capacity is limited. Your choice is limited.'

Charlie sucked away at one of Sammy Jo's robust pink nipples with energetic commitment. Jason tried to expel the random thought that had just entered his head, that often entered his head when he saw Sammy Jo breast-feeding, which was that she seemed like the Madonna when she performed this duty, like an icon, so innocent, uninvolved and natural. He said, 'How long have you had this hang-up about not being free? I thought you were happy to be living with me. I thought you liked being married. I don't think I ever put you under any unnecessary pressure . . .'

Sammy Jo exploded. 'Why does everything have to be so bloody particular with you, Jason? I'm not talking about myself, I'm talking about an idea, a . . .'

She paused and grasped for a word that was brand new and floating around inside her mind, ready to be brought out like the best cutlery at a family celebration. 'I'm talking about universals. A universal idea, freedom. Everything that I say doesn't have to apply to my own miserable life. I can think beyond it, above it, you know. I am just about capable of that.'

He stared at her with his shoulders hunched and his arms crossed defensively, then he said, 'Something's going on, but I don't know what. This isn't like you . . . this isn't you, Sammy Jo.'

She laughed, 'God! Just because I make a slightly intelligent observation you make out something terrible is wrong. You don't think I'm a very clever person, do you, Jason? You don't think I'm particularly blessed with intelligence.'

He looked surprised. 'Of course you're intelligent. I love you, Sammy Jo, I love your mind, your conversation, your body, your beautiful pink nipples, our baby. I do respect you, and I like to think that I treat you as an equal . . .'

She snorted. 'Well thanks a lot for that. I *am* your equal, I don't think you deserve any special thanks for treating me as such.'

Jason leaned over the table and picked up the pizza pad. 'What exactly does this mean, Sammy Jo? "ARE GOOD AND EVIL OF IMPORTANCE TO THE UNIVERSE OR ONLY TO MAN?" BERTRAND RUSSELL. THINK ABOUT THIS. What does it mean? Why have you written it down? Who told you to write it down?' He ripped the page away from the pad and screwed it up in his hand.

Sammy Jo prised Charlie's gums away from her nipple and pulled her shirt together to cover her breasts. Charlie yelled and then started to cry. Sammy Jo stood up, thrust Charlie into Jason's arms and said, 'You bloody feed her. How dare you screw up my notes like that? It's none of your business what I do. I'm not affecting you in any way.' She picked up the ball of crumpled paper from the floor and held it, clenched possessively in her hand. Jason was bouncing Charlie up and down in his arms, trying to calm her down. He stared at Sammy Jo but didn't say anything. After a minute or so Charlie's crying evaporated into breathy whimpers. Jason took her over to her cot and placed her gently into it. Sammy Jo felt like running upstairs to their bedroom in order to curtail this conversation, but she wanted to carry on reading her book, she didn't want to just sit up there sulking, with nothing to do. Jason stood up straight and turned to face Sammy Jo. He crossed his arms. 'This reminds me of something, Sammy Jo. This situation reminds me of something.'

She frowned. 'What the hell is that supposed to mean?'

He shrugged. 'Just a hunch. What would you say if I told you that I was going to telephone Lucy Cosbie right now? Maybe she could shed some light on this thing? You've been strange since she telephoned you the other day.'

Sammy Jo shook her head. 'You're barking up the wrong tree, Jason. Lucy Cosbie has nothing whatever to do with this.'

Jason walked over to the television and switched it off then sat down on the sofa where Sammy Jo had been sitting before. He looked up at her, 'Can't we talk about this sensibly, Sammy Jo? It's no big deal. We don't have to row about it.'

Sammy Jo leaned against the table and looked petulant. 'You said it, Jason. I don't know what your problem is all of a sudden.'

He patted the seat next to him on the sofa. 'Sammy Jo, something is upsetting you or influencing you. I can't quite put my finger on it, but you've said some strange things lately, you seem distant and preoccupied, like something's upsetting you.'

She looked into his face as he spoke and saw that his brown eyes were weary and that his face was drawn. As she looked at him she felt as though she hadn't seen him properly for a long time. She moved and sat down beside him. After a short silence she said, 'I don't want you to get upset, I want you to understand. I don't want any overreactions, all right?'

He stared at her, frowning. She continued. 'Someone's been telephoning me over the past few days . . .'

Jason inhaled deeply. She saw his hands clench into fists.

'Jason, don't get upset. This man isn't like the other one, he's different. He doesn't want to cause trouble, he isn't rude or anything . . . it isn't like that at all.'

Jason spoke, and his voice was low and quiet, 'He telephoned earlier, right? That wasn't your mother at all, was it? You lied to me, Sammy Jo.'

Sammy Jo shook her head. 'It's not like that. I didn't want to upset you. I knew you'd overreact, I knew you'd blow it out of all proportion. It isn't like how it was before, not at all.'

He stared at her. His face seemed very close and long and mean. 'Well how exactly is it now, Sammy Jo? How is it possible for an anonymous caller to be anything other than offensive?'

She shrugged and fiddled momentarily with one of the buttons on her blouse. 'He's teaching me about philosophy. That's all he talks about. Before he phoned I didn't even know what philosophy was, but now he's taught me about Descartes and Sartre and scepticism. I'm reading *The Age of Reason* at the moment and really enjoying it . . .'

Jason sprang up from the sofa and looked down at Sammy Jo from what seemed like a great height.

'How long has this been going on, Sammy Jo? Does Cosbie know about it?'

Sammy Jo looked vulnerable and upset. 'It has nothing at all to do with her, it has nothing to do with you either Jason. It's between him and me. I quite like his calls. They interest me.'

Jason let out a sharp yell of frustration and raised his eyes and hands towards the ceiling as though pleading with an invisible God. 'Sammy Jo don't you understand anything? Don't you see what's happening here? Don't you understand that it doesn't matter what the hell it is that he says to you on the phone, it doesn't matter whether he's swearing at you are singing Gregorian chants, the issue here is power. Power, do you remember? Can't you remember the endless conversations with Lucy and I about why it is that people telephone other people anonymously and abuse their time and their privacy? It's a power thing. He's making you passive. You don't question him, he is in control, he is powerful and you are passive. He probably gets exactly the same kick out of it as if you were involved in some sort of direct, sick, sado-masochistic relationship. He's dictating your life, Sammy Jo, can't you see that? Can't you?'

As he finished speaking he leaned towards her and snatched hold of her arm. She didn't meet his gaze, her arm hung limp in his hand. After several seconds she said quietly, 'You think I don't know all this, don't you? You think I'm so bloody stupid. Well you're wrong. I know all about this shit. Maybe you think that I actually enjoy being dominated, that I actually go out of my way to get into situations where I can be dominated . . .'

Jason dropped her arm, 'What do you expect me to think, Sammy Jo? Do you expect me to congratulate you on getting an education? Do you expect me to go to night classes to learn French so I can discuss Sartre with you in the original? What the hell do you expect me to feel? Pleased? Delighted? Grateful?'

Sammy Jo sprang up and pushed Jason in the chest with her flat hand. 'Don't you dare patronize me, you bastard. How dare you speak to me like this? I'll do what the hell I like with my time and you can't stop me. You just resent him because he is offering me something that you have never bothered offering me.'

Jason laughed. It sounded like the wail of an angry hyena. 'So you think I'm threatened by this pervert do you? You think I'm intimidated by some sick bastard who gets his kicks out of telephoning vulnerable women and talking about philosophy with them?

32

Look at me, Sammy Jo, I'm not threatened, I'm angry. You should
be angry too.'

Sammy Jo pushed past him and marched over to the cot. She lifted
Charlie up with one hand and reached under the mattress with her
other hand. She grabbed hold of her three new books and then
replaced the baby on top of her blankets. Jason watched all of this in
silence and then said harshly, 'Well, that's very mature, Sammy Jo,
hiding books under the baby's mattress, very adult. You thrive on
this sort of deception, don't you? You love your little secrets, your
private collusions.'

Sammy Jo marched past him and towards the door. 'I'm going
upstairs for a while. I don't want to be disturbed.'

Jason slammed his fist down hard on to the table, the force of
which caused a coffee cup, the telephone and pizza pad to jump up
into the air by almost an inch. The telephone made a little jangling,
ringing noise as it landed. He yelled, 'Give me those books Sammy
Jo, give them to me now!'

She held her books against her chest and glared at him venomously. 'You'll have to kill me first, Jason. Be warned, I'm not quite
as passive as you'd like to believe.'

They stared at each other venomously for several seconds and
then Sammy Jo turned and left the room.

In the kitchen the ratatouille was starting to burn. Jason switched
off the oven and started to prepare a bottle for the baby. His hands
were shaking.

After forty-five minutes Jason had fed the baby and watched half
of *Coronation Street*. He kept listening out for any noises from
upstairs, but the house was silent. He switched the television off,
opened his briefcase and took out his address book. He found Lucy
Cosbie's number and dialled it. It rang several times before she
answered it.

'Hi, Lucy here.'

Her voice was depressingly familiar to him. He said, 'Hello, Lucy,
it's Jason Wells here, Sammy Jo's husband.'

This took Lucy Cosbie several seconds to register, then she

responded warmly: 'Oh, Jason, hi. Is something wrong? You're the last person I expected to hear from.'

Jason cleared his throat. 'Lucy, Sammy Jo's in trouble again. She said you phoned her the other day. I wondered whether she'd told you about it. I'm somewhat concerned.'

Lucy Cosbie sounded mystified. 'Jason, Sammy Jo said nothing to me about any problems. Is it the baby?'

Jason smiled. 'No, nothing like that. I'm afraid she's receiving anonymous calls again.'

Lucy responded sharply. 'Who from? Same guy?'

Jason was surprised. 'No, I don't think so. She didn't suggest to me that it could be the same person. I think she would've said that. I hope so anyway.'

Lucy breathed a sigh of relief. 'I'm glad to hear that, Jason. It's all a bit complicated at this end because I've seen a fair bit of him lately. I was assigned to his case recently. I'm sure you can understand that it's something of a conflict of interests.'

Jason nodded. 'I can imagine. Anyway, Lucy, this new guy is really weird, they aren't dirty calls as such. In fact Sammy Jo seems very happy with the arrangement. It seems that he's teaching her philosophy, you know, "Philosophy the Anonymous Caller's Way".'

He tried to crack this joke light-heartedly but it fell somewhat flat. Lucy Cosbie was silent for a few seconds and then she said, rather slowly and hollowly, 'Oh dear. I think this could all be slightly problematic.'

Jason scratched his head and then tightened his grip on the telephone receiver. 'Why? I didn't think what was said made any difference. He's still pestering her. It's the same thing isn't it? The same as before?'

When Lucy next spoke she sounded a fraction testy. 'Jason, I think maybe I should speak to Sammy Jo about this. Is she there? Can I have a word?'

Jason was irritated. 'She's upstairs at the moment. We've had a slight disagreement about the whole thing. She's being a bit irrational.'

Lucy was persistent. 'I'm sorry Jason, I'm afraid that I can't talk to you any further about this without chatting to Sammy Jo. I'd prefer to deal with her personally. I'd appreciate it if I could speak with her privately.'

Jason frowned. After a short pause he said, 'I'll go and call her. I don't know how responsive she'll be though. Hang on.'

He put down the telephone and walked into the hallway. He stood at the bottom of the stairs and shouted up, 'Sammy Jo? Lucy Cosbie's on the phone, she wants to speak to you.'

Sammy Jo was lying on their bed engrossed in her book. She swore under her breath at Jason's untimely interruption and turned over the corner of the page to mark her place. She got up and shouted back as she began to make her way towards the door. 'I'm coming!'

As she walked down the stairs she glared at him. 'I bet you phoned her.' He shrugged as she brushed past him and decided that it was probably better to say nothing.

Sammy Jo picked up the telephone. 'Hi Lucy, I'm sorry about this. I'm sure you've got more pressing matters to deal with. This isn't at all important.'

Lucy's voice was low and apologetic. 'Sammy Jo, I'm sorry, but I do think that this is my business. I'm pretty sure that I know who it is that's telephoning you and also how and why.'

Sammy Jo frowned. 'I don't understand.'

Lucy sighed. 'I think it's my fault. I've been a bit slow on the uptake. Maybe I haven't been careful enough. That man, Duncan Sands, who was telephoning you before, well, he was recently assigned to me . . .'

Sammy Jo interrupted nervously. 'I thought he was in prison.'

'No, he was in an open prison for several months but he's been out for a while now. You were hardly the only person involved in the whole mess . . . well, you know all about it, anyway.'

Sammy Jo shook her head slowly while she listened to Lucy. 'I'm sorry Lucy, but this person is different, they aren't the same, they don't sound the same.'

Lucy was insistent. 'Sammy Jo, he may not sound the same because he's saying different things, but I know it's him. He often asks about you. He wanted to meet you a while back to talk things over. He sincerely believes that he's better now, that he was sick and now he's better. I somehow have my doubts about that. Anyway, he's been heavily involved in community service work and maybe he thinks that he's doing you some sort of a service. He started a sociology course in prison and he's really into educating himself. I helped to get him a job a few weeks back, only part-time shop work, but with prospects. Next year, if they keep him on, he'll probably be eligible for a day-release scheme to go to the polytechnic. He wants to get a degree in Communication Studies.'

Sammy Jo laughed. 'I suppose that's kind of ironic.'

Lucy wasn't amused. 'He must've managed to find out your number from me at some point. I don't know, maybe he got a peek at my diary or something. Anyway Sammy Jo, I'm going to have to do something about this . . .'

Sammy Jo bit her lip. 'Lucy, you aren't going to tell the police are you? Or jeopardize his job?'

Lucy was silent for a moment and then she said, 'He's violated my trust, Sammy Jo. I have a responsibility to do something.'

Sammy Jo interrupted angrily. 'That's stupid! It's none of your business. You'd never have known about this if Jason hadn't told you. As far as I'm concerned, his involvement with me is with my full consent.'

Lucy tutted irritatingly. 'Sammy Jo, you know it's not as simple as that. This whole anonymous calling thing is about power, it doesn't matter what he's saying, it's wrong. We both know that it's wrong.'

Sammy Jo said slyly, 'You let him get my number, Lucy, that was irresponsible, what if I wanted to make something of it?'

Lucy wasn't impressed. 'That makes no difference to me, Sammy Jo, I don't intend to follow one piece of misconduct with another.'

Sammy Jo wound the telephone wire around her middle finger and tried to think of some sort of compromise. Eventually she said, 'Lucy, I swear to you that if he telephones me again I'll phone you and tell you, then you can contact whoever you like. Just leave it until the next time. Maybe you could phone him tonight and warn him off . . .'

Lucy sounded impatient. 'I don't know, Sammy Jo. I don't think my telling him will change his modes of behaviour. I don't know if I can trust you on this either. You haven't been particularly co-operative up until this point.'

Sammy Jo raised her eyebrows and pulled an innocently sly expression. 'I realize that, Lucy. I know that this isn't just about me and that I have a wider responsibility, but I also know that he deserves a chance to make a go of his job in the bookshop, especially since his prospects seem to be looking up . . .'

Lucy sounded surprised. 'Did I mention that he was working in a bookshop? I don't think I said that, did I?'

Sammy Jo shrugged, but she was smiling to herself. 'Forget it Lucy, I'm just a bit stressed out. I promise though, this time you can depend on me, really.'

They rang off. Jason had come into the room during the final stages of their conversation and was sitting on the sofa staring at Sammy Jo inquisitively. Sammy Jo sat down next to him and took hold of his hand. 'It's all right, I'm not angry. I've cleared it all up with Lucy. I don't think he'll be phoning me again.'

Jason squeezed her fingers and kissed her cheek. 'Sammy Jo, if you want to go to college you could always go in the evenings and I'll look after Charlie. I wouldn't mind. Maybe we could give her to a babyminder a couple of days a week and you could go on a course part-time.'

Sammy Jo shrugged. 'I don't know, Jason, I don't think I'm ready for that yet. I don't feel brave enough. I like being at home with Charlie at the moment, I just appreciate the occasional bit of stimulation. I'm really enjoying this book I'm reading, and there's no pressure, you know, no need to take exams or to get along with a classful of strangers . . .'

Jason smiled. 'You know that you can do anything that you want to do, Sammy Jo. I know that you'll choose whatever is for the best.'

Sammy Jo smiled back.

*

The following morning at ten o'clock Sammy Jo picked up her copy of the Yellow Pages and hunted down a number. When she had located it she opened up her new pad and wrote the number down at the top of the first large, white page in big bold print. Then she picked up the telephone and dialled. When someone answered she smiled and said, 'Hello, this is Sammy Jo, remember me? Yes, I know you're at work, yes I know you're busy, but I don't care. Maybe you should give me your home number and then I wouldn't have to pester you like this . . .'

The line went dead. She put down her receiver, picked it up again and then pressed the redial button. She waited for a moment and then continued. 'Yes, it is me again. No, I don't care what sort of a disruption this is. I want to carry on our conversations. Apparently you're working part-time? That means you must have a lot of spare time on your hands during the afternoons, which is good, good for me at any rate. I want you to share that free time with me, on the phone of course, reverse charges. I've been thinking about that question you asked me yesterday, I'd like to discuss it at greater length . . .'

The line went dead. She put down her receiver and then picked it up and, once again, pressed redial. 'You're an old hand at this, Mr Sands, I have a redial button and it's no effort to press it again and again . . .'

She listened for a moment, then picked up her pen and copied down another number in her white pad. Then she said, 'Yes, I am enjoying it actually . . . No, I didn't tell Lucy, someone else did . . . No, Lucy didn't tell me either, it didn't take much intelligence to realize though . . . Thank you. Is two o'clock all right? OK, I'll phone you then. Goodbye.'

She hung up.

The Butcher's Apprentice

If he had come from a family of butchers maybe his perspective would have been different. He would have been more experienced, hardened, less naïve. His mum had wanted him to work for Marks and Spencers or for British Rail. She said, 'Why do you want to work in all that blood and mess? There's something almost obscene about butchery.'

His dad was more phlegmatic. 'It's not like cutting the Sunday roast, Owen, it's guts and gore and entrails. Just the same, it's a real trade, a proper trade.'

Owen had thought it all through. At school one of his teachers had called him 'deep'. She had said to his mother on Parents' Evening, 'Owen seems deep, but it's hard to get any sort of real response from him. Maybe it's just cosmetic.'

His mum had listened to the first statement but had then become preoccupied with a blister on the heel of her right foot. Consequently her grasp of the teacher's wisdom had been somewhat undermined. When she finally got home that evening, her stomach brimming with sloshy coffee from the school canteen, she had said to Owen, 'Everyone says that you're too quiet at school, but your maths teacher thinks that you're deep. She has modern ideas, that one.' Owen had appreciated this compliment. It made him try harder at maths that final term before his exams, and leaving. At sixteen he had pass marks in mathematics, home economics and the whole world before him.

In the Careers Office his advisor had given him a leaflet about prospective employment opportunities to fill out. He ticked various boxes. He ticked a yes for 'Do you like working with your hands?' He ticked a yes for 'Do you like working with animals?' He ticked a yes for 'Do you like using your imagination?'

When his careers guidance officer had analysed his preferences she declared that his options were quite limited. He seemed such a quiet boy to her, rather dour. She said, 'Maybe you could be a postman. Postmen see a lot of animals during their rounds and use their hands to deliver letters.' Owen appeared unimpressed. He stared down at his hands as though they had suddenly become a cause for embarrassment. So she continued, 'Maybe you could think about working with food. How about training to be a chef or a butcher? Butchers work with animals. You have to use your imagination to make the right cut into a carcass.' Because he had been in the careers office for well over half an hour, Owen began to feel obliged to make some sort of positive response. A contribution. So he looked up at her and said, 'Yeah, I suppose I could give it a try.' He didn't want to appear stroppy or ungrateful. She smiled at him and gave him an address. The address was for J. Reilly and Sons, Quality Butchers, 103 Oldham Road.

Later that afternoon he phoned J. Reilly's and spoke to someone called Ralph. Ralph explained how he had bought the business two years before, but that he hadn't bothered changing the name. Owen said, 'Well, if it doesn't bother you then it doesn't bother me.'

Ralph asked him a few questions about school and then enquired whether he had worked with meat before. Owen said that he hadn't but that he really liked the sweet smell of a butcher's shop and the scuffling sawdust on the floor, the false plastic parsley in the window displays and the bright, blue-tinged strip-lights. He said, 'I think that I could be very happy in a butcher's as a working environment.'

He remembered how as a child he had so much enjoyed seeing the arrays of different coloured rabbits hung up by their ankles in butcher shop windows, and the bright and golden-speckled pheasants. Ralph offered him a month's probationary employment with a view to a full-time apprenticeship. Owen accepted readily.

His mum remained uncertain. Over dinner that night she said, 'It'll be nice to get cheap meat and good cuts from your new job, Owen, though I still don't like the idea of a butcher in the family. I've nothing against them in principal, but it's different when it's so close to home.'

Owen thought carefully for a moment, then put aside his knife and fork and said, 'I suppose so, but that's only on the surface. I'm sure that there's a lot of bloodletting and gore involved in most occupations. I like the idea of being honest and straightforward about things. A butcher is a butcher. There's no falseness or pretence.'

His dad nodded his approval and then said, 'Eat up now, don't let your dinner get cold.'

Owen arrived at the shop at seven sharp the following morning. The window displays were whitely clean and empty. Above the windows the J. Reilly and Sons sign was painted in red with white lettering. The graphics were surprisingly clear and ornate. On the door was hung a sign which said 'closed'. He knocked anyway. A man with arms like thin twigs opened the door. He looked tiny and consumptive with shrewd grey eyes and rusty hair. Owen noticed his hands, which were reddened with the cold, calloused and porkish. The man nodded briskly, introduced himself as Ralph then took Owen through to the back of the shop and introduced him to his work-mate, Marty. Marty was older than Ralph – about fifty or so – with silvery hair and yellow skin. He smiled at Owen kindly and offered him a clean apron and a bag of sawdust. Owen took the apron and placed it over his head. Ralph helped him to tie at the back. Both Marty and Ralph wore overalls slightly more masculine in design. Owen took the bag of sawdust and said, 'Is this a woman's apron, or is it what the apprentice always wears?'

As Ralph walked back into the main part of the shop he answered, 'It belongs to our Saturday girl, so don't get it too messy. We'll buy you a proper overall at the end of the week when we're sure that you're right for the job.'

As he finished speaking a large van drew up outside the shop. Ralph moved to the door, pulled it wide and stuck a chip of wood under it to keep it open. He turned to Owen and by way of explanation pointed and said, 'Delivery. The meat's brought twice a week. Scatter the sawdust, but not too thick.'

Owen put his hand into the bag of dust and drew out a full, dry, scratchy handful which he scattered like a benevolent farmer throwing corn to his geese. The delivery man humped in half of an emormous sow. She had a single greenish eye and a severed snout. He took it to the back of the shop through a door and into what Owen presumed to be the refrigerated store-room. Before he had returned Ralph had come in clutching a large armful of plucked chickens. As Owen moved out of his way he nodded towards the van and said, 'I tell you what, why not go and grab some stuff yourself but don't overestimate your strength and try not to drop anything.'

Owen balanced his packet of shavings against the bottom of the counter and walked out to the van. Inside were a multitude of skins, feathers, meats and flesh. He grabbed four white rabbits and a large piece of what he presumed to be pork, but later found out was lamb. The meat was fresh and raw to the touch. Raw and soft like risen dough. He lifted his selections out of the van and carried them into the shop, careful of the condition of his apron, and repeated this process back and forth for the next fifteen or so minutes. While everyone else moved the meat, Marty busied himself with cutting steaks from a large chunk of beef. When finally all of the meat had been moved Ralph went and had a cigarette outside with the delivery man and Owen picked up his bag of shavings and finished scattering them over the shop floor. On completing this he called over to Marty, 'Do I have to spread this on the other side of the counter as well?'

Marty smiled at him. 'I think that's the idea. It should only take you a minute, so when you've finished come over here and see what I'm doing. You never know, you might even learn something.'

Owen quickly tipped out the rest of his bag over the floor at the back of the counter and scuffed the dust around with his foot. It covered the front of his trainer like a light, newgrown beard. Then he walked over to Marty and stood at his shoulder watching him complete his various insertions into the beef. Marty made his final cut and then half turned and showed Owen the blade he was using. He moved the tip of the blade adjacent to the tip of Owen's nose. 'A blade has to be sharp. That's the first rule of butchery. Rule two, your hands must be clean.' He moved the knife from side to side and

Owen's eyes followed its sharp edge. It was so close to his face that he could see his hot breath steaming up and evaporating on its steely surface. Marty said thickly, 'This blade could slice your nose in half in the time it takes you to sneeze. Aaah-tish-yooouh!'

Then he whipped the knife away and placed it carefully on the cutting surface next to a small pool of congealing blood. He said, 'Rule three, treat your tools with respect.'

Owen cleared his throat self-consciously. 'Will I be allowed to cut up some meat myself today, or will I just be helping out around the shop?' Marty frowned. 'It takes a long time and a lot of skill to be able to prepare meat properly. You'll have to learn everything from scratch. That's what it means to be the new boy, the apprentice.'

Ralph came back into the shop and set Owen to work cleaning the insides of the windows and underneath the display trays. Old blood turned the water brown. Soon the first customers of the day started to straggle into the shop and he learned the art of pricing and weighing. The day moved on. At twelve he had half-an-hour for lunch.

After two o'clock the shop quietened down again and Owen was sent into the store-room to acquaint himself with the lay-out, refrigeration techniques and temperatures. As he looked around and smelt the heavy, heady smell of ripe meat, he overheard Ralph and Marty laughing at something in the shop. Ralph was saying, 'Leave him be. You're wicked Mart.' Marty replied, 'He won't mind. Go on, it'll be a laugh.'

A few seconds later Ralph called through to him. Owen walked into the shop from the cool darkness of the storeroom. The light made his eyes squint. The shop was empty apart from Ralph and Marty who were standing together in front of the large cutting board as though hiding something. Ralph said, 'Have you ever seen flesh, dead flesh, return to life, Owen?' Owen shook his head. Marty smiled at him. 'Some meat is possessed, you know. If a live animal is used as part of a satanic ritual at any point during its life, when it dies its flesh lives on to do the devil's work. After all, the devil's work is never done.'

As he finished speaking he stepped sideways to reveal a large chunk of fleshy meat on the chopping board. It was about the size of a cabbage. Everyone stared at it. They were all silent. Slowly, gradually, almost imperceptibly, the meat shuddered. Owen blinked to make sure that his eyes were clear and not deceiving him. After a couple of seconds it shuddered again, but this time more noticeably. It shivered as though it were too cold, and then slowly, painfully, began to crawl across the table. It moved like a heart that pumped under great duress, a struggling, battling, palpitating heart.

Owen's face blanched. His throat tightened. Ralph and Marty watched his initial reactions and then returned their gazes to the flesh. By now it had moved approximately five or six inches across the cutting board. Its motions were those of a creature in agony, repulsive and yet full of an agonizing pathos. Owen felt his eyes fill, he felt like howling.

Ralph turned back to look at Owen and saw, with concern, the intensity of his reactions. He said, 'Don't get all upset, it's only a joke. It's got nothing to do with the devil, honest.'

He smiled. Owen frowned and swallowed hard before attempting to reply. 'Why is it moving? What have you done to it?'

Marty reached towards the piece of convulsing flesh with his big butcher's hand and picked it up. As he lifted it the flesh seemed to cling to the table. It made a noise like wet clay being ripped into two pieces, like a limpet being pulled from its rock. He turned it over. Underneath, inside, permeating the piece of meat, was a huge round cancer the size of Marty's fist. A miracle tumour, complete, alive. The tumour was contracting and then relaxing, contracting and relaxing. Maybe it was dying. Owen stared at the tumour in open-mouthed amazement, at its orangy, yellowy completeness, its outside and its core. Marty said, 'Sometimes the abattoir send us a carcass that shouldn't really be for human consumption. They know that an animal is ill but they slaughter it just before it dies. They have to make a living too, I suppose.'

With that he threw the meat and its cancerous centre into a large half-full refuse bag and began to wipe over the work surface as though nothing had happened. Owen could still make out the movements of the cancer from inside the bag. A customer came into the shop and Ralph walked over to serve her. Owen felt overwhelmed by a great sense of injustice, a feeling of enormous intensity, unlike anything he had ever experienced before. He felt as though his insides were tearing. He felt appalled. Then instinctively he grabbed at the back of his apron and yanked open its bow. He pulled it over his head and slammed it on to the counter. He said, 'I'm going home now. I'm going home and I'm taking this with me.'

Before anyone could respond Owen had grabbed the heavy refuse bag full of bones and gristle and off-cuts and had struggled his way out of the shop. When he had gone, Ralph turned to Marty and said, 'He was a nice enough kid.'

Marty shrugged.

Owen got out of the shop and walked a short distance down the road before placing the bag on the pavement and opening it. He reached inside and felt for the cancer. When he finally touched it, it sucked on his finger like a fish or a baby. He took it out of the bag, pulled off his sweater and bundled the cancer up inside it. He carried it on the bus as though it were a sick puppy. It moved very slightly. When he got home he crept upstairs and locked himself in his room. He closed the curtains and then sat on his bed and unbundled the tumour. He placed it gently on his bedside table under the warm glow of his lamp. It was growing weaker and now moved only slowly.

Owen wondered what he could do for it. He debated whether to pour water on it or whether to try and keep it warm. He wondered whether it might be kinder to kill it quickly, but he couldn't work out how. He wondered if you could drown a tumour (that would be painless enough), or whether you could chop it in half. But he couldn't be sure that tumours weren't like the amoebas that he'd studied in biology at school that could divide and yet still survive. He couldn't really face destroying it. Instead he decided to simply stay with it and to offer it moral support. He whispered quietly, 'Come on, it'll be all right. It'll soon be over.'

After a few hours the tumour was only moving intermittently. Its movements had grown sluggish and irregular. Owen stayed with it.

He kept it company. He chatted. Eventually the tumour stopped moving altogether. Its meaty exterior was completely still. He knew that it was dead. He picked it up tenderly and cradled it in his arms as he carried it downstairs, out of the house and into the garden. Placing it gently on the grass, he dragged at the soft soil in the flowerbeds with both his hands until he had dug a hole of significant proportions. Then he placed the still tumour into the hole and covered it over. In a matter of minutes the soil was perfectly compacted and the flowerbed looked as normal.

He went inside and lay on his bed awhile. At six he went downstairs to the kitchen where his mother was beginning to prepare dinner. As he poured himself a glass of water she said, 'I didn't know that you were home. How did your first day go?'

Owen gulped down the water and then placed his glass upside down on the draining board. He said, 'I think I'm going to be a postman.'

Then he dried his hands on a kitchen towel and asked what was for dinner.

Skin

Stephanie was over fifteen minutes late. Jane sat in a window-seat and read her paperback (bought for exactly this kind of occasion), intermittently sipping her half pint of lager.

They had arranged to meet in the Red Lion at seven o'clock. Jane hated sitting in pubs alone, she felt conspicuous, although in fact she was no more conspicuous than any woman who sat in a pub alone might be. She was reading an early Jilly Cooper which she had bought second-hand from a book stall outside the Festival Hall during the previous summer.

In general (since her 'A' levels) she had preferred to read magazines rather than novels, but in certain situations she felt that magazines created an unnecessarily promiscuous impression. Girls on the tube who read them often had long, painted fingernails, smart shoes and sheer tights. Magazines represented a disposable lifestyle; Jane preferred the idea of an indispensable lifestyle: at twenty-four, she worked in a bank and was rather conservative.

She looked up from her novel and stared momentarily out of the window – through a pair of yellowy nets – hoping to catch a glimpse of Stephanie trotting down the road towards her, but instead, all she saw was the reflection of a nearby street-light in the glass of the window, a bleary, streaky, visual sludge. Her eyes returned to the words on the page.

The pub was empty apart from two men slouching at the bar, a young couple, who seemed to be recovering from a recent argument, sitting in an alcove, and over towards the door a pensioner who was reading a late edition of the *Evening Standard*. Someone had put some money into the juke box, which was playing 'Suspicious Minds'. Jane imagined that it might have been the male half of the young couple.

As her eyes sped across the page, Jane thought for a moment

about her boyfriend Mitch and Stephanie's boyfriend Chris. She wondered what they were doing. Maybe they were watching the football on television, or maybe they were playing snooker.

The pub's doors swung open. Everybody turned towards them. Jane had earlier been engaged in a heated debate with herself about how to react when the doors opened. Initially she had decided that it was best if she ignored the various comings and goings around her. She had endeavoured to create the impression of calculated indifference, preoccupation, oblivion. Later, however, she had decided that it might be appropriate to look up fleetingly from her book towards the door so that people who might be looking at her would know immediately that the only reason for her continuing presence in the pub was the fact that she was waiting for someone. She was expecting someone. It made her feel less vulnerable, also less approachable.

On this occasion she was glad that she had looked up. Stephanie stood in the doorway, looking ruffled and indecisive. Jane waved at her and smiled. Stephanie caught her eye, smiled back, relieved, then pointed her finger towards the bar. Jane nodded. Stephanie then pointed a finger towards Jane's drink. Jane shook her head and placed a prim, flat hand over the top of her glass. Stephanie walked to the bar and ordered a gin and tonic.

Jane watched her, at last relaxing in the pub's worn, red velvet environs, putting down her book and leaning back in her chair. She watched Stephanie as she waited for her drink and then paid for it. Stephanie was still wearing her uniform – she worked in John Lewis, the Oxford Street branch – and her hair was tied back in a ponytail. She looked young for twenty-four. Jane thought it must be the way that she had tied back her hair. As Stephanie approached her Jane said ironically, 'I'm surprised the barman served you, Steph, you don't look eighteen with your hair tied back like that.'

Stephanie put her spirits glass down and squeezed in between the table and the seat. As she sat down she touched her hair with a free hand and looked unnecessarily self-conscious, then said, 'I think the barman'd serve a large squirrel if it appeared at the counter and asked for a pint of lager. He doesn't look too discriminating.'

Jane shrugged. Stephanie pointed towards Jane's book. 'Jilly Cooper. Good?'

Jane picked up the book and put it into her bag. 'Something to read. It's not like you to be late.'

Stephanie frowned, 'I know. I've had a bit of a strange day. Sorry.'

Jane raised her eyebrows, professionally interested. 'Busy?'

Stephanie shrugged. 'Not too bad. You?'

Jane shook her head. 'So so.'

They both picked up their drinks and took a sip. On returning her glass to the table Stephanie put her hands to the back of her head and pulled her hairband out. She then shook free her hair which fell about her shoulders in semi-curls. Jane watched her as she did this and couldn't help thinking that Stephanie was looking particularly well, strangely spruce, as though she had just had a shower, an odd post-swimming clean-washed look. She sniffed the air for a trace of chlorine but could smell none. 'You haven't been swimming, have you? Marshall Street pool?'

Stephanie looked guilty, 'No. Well, yes. Well, I had a shower, that's all.'

Jane frowned. 'Where's your towel? Why did you have a shower? That's odd. Are you wearing any make-up? Why did you have a shower?'

Stephanie looked overwhelmed, 'I . . . I needed a shower. I hired a towel.'

Jane began to pull a fastidious expression.

'Honestly, it was perfectly clean.' Stephanie's face crumpled. 'Oh God! I feel . . . I don't know. I was going to say I feel awful, but in fact I feel almost the opposite.' She thought for a moment. 'I feel rather, almost hysterical. Pent up. I've done the strangest thing.'

Jane was frowning. 'Is everything all right at work?'

Stephanie nodded wordlessly.

'Chris? Nothing's happened between you and Chris?'

Stephanie shook her head, 'No, Chris is fine.' She frowned. 'I don't feel as if I can tell you . . .'

Jane clucked her tongue, exasperated. 'What can't you tell me? You always tell me everything. What's going on?'

*

They had been best friends since primary school. Jane had always been dominant and Stephanie softer, better intentioned but easily swayed. She saw life as a set of rules which she obeyed. Jane saw life as a set of rules which she supported. She thought Stephanie's passivity occasionally subversive, but knew her well enough to be sure of her back-up and understanding in most situations. They came from the same stock, a simmering, warm if unadventurous stew of suburban values; their schooling the same, parents the same, boyfriends the same, and their ambitions . . . ?

Jane stared at Stephanie across the table and wondered what it was that she had done. She shoved around a set of geometric boundaries in her mind, a variety of fully contained and containable possibilities. 'Pregnant?'

Stephanie grimaced. She looked up at Jane and felt almost helpless; she must tell her because who else could she tell? (God knows, not her mother.) And the notion of saying nothing was virtually inconceivable. She knew that all acts suffered in the doing because of the inevitability of the telling. She must tell her.

Jane watched, waiting. Stephanie took a further sip of her drink, laced her hands together on her lap and then took a deep breath. 'I'm downstairs in the Men's Knitwear Department this week, occasionally on the till, but mainly involved with stock, pricing, you know . . .'

Jane nodded, she had a picture of the knitwear department in her mind, and a cardigan that she wanted to buy for Mitch. 'Knitwear Department. So?'

Stephanie looked down at her hands. 'Well, I was . . . It was dead during the last hour, you know how it can be, hardly anyone about, and I was tidying up, straightening jumpers on hangers and refolding . . . I don't know if it's the same in the bank, but the last hour is always the worst and the best, the way the minute-hand keeps you in but the hour-hand points towards the door . . .'

Jane was nonplussed by Stephanie's attempts to wax lyrical. 'The last hour. Right.'

Stephanie took a deep breath. She knew this wasn't going to be easy. 'I was folding up some vests and socks when I noticed a man near by, well, I think that initially there were two of them, but the other one wandered off. They were skins, really tall in puffy green jackets and tight, short jeans and boots . . .'

Jane frowned. 'White trash.'

Stephanie bit her lip and nodded. 'Really short hair, just like, just really short, soft, like a coloured shadow on the scalp. But smart, not like normal skins, with bleached trousers and tatoos on their necks, like ugly roosters, dirty. This one was smart . . .'

Jane reiterated her earlier point, which made a class distinction as opposed to a value judgement. 'White trash. Yuk. Shoplifting I bet. Pringle jumpers or long socks for under their boots.'

Stephanie nodded. 'Socks.'

She was silent for a moment. In her mind she outlined what she was going to say and felt her stomach contract with the extremity of it. She thought momentarily of not telling and then knew that she must tell. She tried a different approach. 'Do you ever have that feeling sometimes when everything feels sort of, strong, like soup or evaporated milk, sort of condensed, as though some things just must happen in a specific way, like a recipe . . . ?'

Jane looked uncomprehending, 'Like what? No, I don't think so.'

Stephanie frowned. 'Like when you first fell in love with Mitch, like when you first decided to have your hair cut, or the feeling you get when you want to dive into a pool but know that the water is cold, but you want to dive in anyway.'

Jane sipped her lager and watched as one of the men at the bar walked over and put some money into the juke box. Doris Day started singing 'Move Over Darling'. She tapped her foot in time and tried to respond appropriately to what Stephanie was saying.

'I don't know what you mean. Did you go swimming after all? Why all this talk about swimming all of a sudden?'

Stephanie looked crestfallen. She knew that she was already losing Jane's sympathy. 'That was a simile. Remember? Like Gerard Manley Hopkins or someone. I was trying to explain a feeling.'

Jane rolled her eyes. 'Just tell me what you *mean*. What about that skinhead, the shoplifter. Did you catch him?'

Stephanie nodded. 'Yes, I caught him.'

'And then?' Jane drained her glass of lager and placed it decisively down on a beermat. Stephanie studied her own glass, watched the condensation on the exterior of its bowl and around its base. The glass left a ring of moisture on the surface of the table when she picked it up. She took a sip and replaced it, but in a different place so that she could study the damp ring on the table's surface, moisten her finger in the dampness and then draw on the polished wood. She drew another circle. 'I walked over to him and told him that I knew he had placed some socks inside his jacket. I asked whether he intended to pay for them.'

'What did he say? Didn't you try and call the store detective? I would have.'

Stephanie drew two dots inside the circle and then a straight line. The circle was now a face, a round, rather simple but glum-looking face. 'No, I didn't call the store detective. It was almost twenty-to-six. I didn't want the hassle.'

'Weren't you frightened?'

She nodded. 'I suppose so. He was tall. At first he just stared at me. Then he turned, as if he was going to walk away.'

'And then?'

'I put out my hand and grabbed his arm. He had one of those weird jackets on, a puffy green jacket. He must've been almost six feet tall. Mean-looking.'

Jane stopped tapping her foot as the Doris Day song finished on the juke box. She looked over to see if the two young men at the bar were going to put another song on but they had recently been joined by a third man and were deep in conversation. Stephanie smiled at her. 'Can I get you another drink yet?'

Jane shook her head. 'Not yet. Wait a while. So what happened then?'

Stephanie looked down at the table again, at the face she had drawn, which was already evaporating. She picked up some more moistness from the ring left by the glass and cut across the face with several rapid strokes. 'I took hold of his arm and said, "You can't leave here until you put those socks back." He grinned at me and said, "Which socks? I haven't got any."'

'Did he pull his arm away?'

Stephanie looked disconcerted. 'Um. No. I don't think he pulled his arm away. It was all very quick. The aisle was empty. The whole shop seemed empty.'

'What did you say then?'

Stephanie took another sip of her drink. 'I said, "You have got socks there, I saw you pick them up. I'm not stupid. Please just put them back and I'll leave you alone."'

'And did he?'

She shook her head. 'No. He looked down at my hand on his arm and started to smile. He said, "I haven't got any socks, only on my feet." I said, "I know you've got them," and indicated with my other hand towards a bulge in his jacket where I'd seen him put the socks.'

'Why didn't you call one of the store detectives? I'm surprised they didn't notice him come in. Probably on a tea break.'

Jane created her own scenarios; scrupulous and disapproving. Stephanie shrugged. 'I don't know where they were. Anyway, I could handle it. He didn't turn nasty. I think he was surprised. I wouldn't let him go.'

Jane smiled. 'You're small but ferocious, like a terrier. Did he give you the socks?'

Stephanie tried to smile back. 'After a while, yes. He put his hand inside his jacket and produced the socks. He threw them on to the nearest shelf. The shop seemed so quiet. He was still smiling at me.'

Jane wrinkled up her nose. 'Yuk. Creepy.'

Stephanie continued, 'And then he started to apologize. I don't know why. I hadn't expected him to. He started to apologize like he'd offended me somehow. It was strange.'

Jane nodded. 'At least he had some manners. Did you let him go? I would've called the store detectives. I suppose it was too late by then though, but he shouldn't have got away with it. Did he just leave?'

Stephanie took a deep breath. 'Well, while he was apologizing I realized that I still had my hand on his arm. We sort of realized at the same time. And then, and then . . .'

Jane raised her eyebrows, 'And then?'

Stephanie bit her lip. 'Then we, sort of, kissed.'

Jane looked so shocked that Stephanie wanted to laugh, but couldn't quite bring herself to.

'What? A proper kiss? A kiss?'

Stephanie nodded. 'It just happened.'

Jane fought down two competing impulses in her gut, the first of total disapproval, the second of total fascination. Stephanie watched this conflict translate itself on to Jane's face and said, 'It didn't mean anything.'

Finally Jane asked, 'What sort of a kiss? A French kiss? What did you say after?'

Stephanie blushed. 'A French kiss. His mouth tasted of cough sweets and smoke. We didn't really say anything. If he did say something, it was only to apologize about the socks again.'

Jane frowned. 'So what did you do? After?'

Stephanie shrugged. 'I . . . I suppose I put my hand under his shirt. He was wearing a T-shirt.'

'You were looking for more socks? You were, weren't you?'

Stephanie burst out laughing. She had recovered from her earlier embarrassment. 'No. By then I had forgotten about the socks. I was feeling his stomach and his chest. His chest was hairless, but surprisingly firm.'

Jane was silent for a moment, trying to understand what this situation meant. Stephanie had never been a promiscuous person. She stared at her face across the table and looked for any perceptible signs of distress. There were none. After a while she said, 'Why did it happen? You've never done this sort of thing before. I thought you were faithful to Chris. I don't understand you.'

Stephanie sighed. 'I was trying to explain earlier. Of course I've never done anything like this before. It was strange, as though . . . like a compulsion. Inevitable. Dangerous but compulsive. I don't know. I can't understand it myself. It's not as though we were immediately physically attracted. It was more the situation itself, the differences between us . . .'

Jane interrupted. 'I suppose it was only a kiss. Maybe it was just mutual attraction.'

Stephanie looked momentarily indecisive and then said, 'No, that's the whole point. It wasn't just a kiss. We had sex.'

To fill the following silence she added, 'The more I think about it, the more I'm convinced that it was just a power thing. There was something explosive about the situation, the confrontation, something strangely . . . well, strange. Erotic.'

Stephanie looked down at her hands. She had never used the word 'erotic' before. Especially in front of someone like Jane. Using the word was almost as much fun as the sex had been. She felt like D. H. Lawrence.

Jane was devastated. She looked at Stephanie and couldn't understand her, she couldn't contain what she had done in the relevant compartments of her brain. She wondered whether Stephanie was now a slag. A slut. Finally she said, 'You behaved like a slut, with some big, ugly skinhead.'

Stephanie shrugged. 'If you mean "slut" in a good way, then yes, I did. The shop was so quiet. We made love behind some racks of mohair jumpers. Nobody came.'

She smiled at her unintentional pun. Jane missed the joke. Her ideas of Stephanie had now been so radically altered that any coherent discussion about motivation and intent seemed entirely fruitless. But she was like a small, common bird, like a sparrow, a pack creature, something that acts on impulse. She wanted to know the details, but this desire compromised her and she knew it. Eventually she said, 'How was he?' She had never been able to ask this question about the sexual relations between Stephanie and Chris, but this was different. Stephanie looked for a moment like she wasn't going to reply, then she said, 'Good. Strange. Condensed . . .'

'Did he have . . . ?'

Stephanie frowned. 'Don't ask. It wasn't like that.'

Jane felt coarse and embarrassed. She snapped defensively, 'I'm not particularly interested in what it was like. Don't flatter yourself.'

She was silent for a second and then added, 'How can we even discuss it? How can we talk about it? There's nothing to say.'

Stephanie frowned, trying to understand what Jane meant. She said, 'I thought I should tell you.'

Jane raised her eyebrows and tried to look ironic. 'Tell me? Tell me what? I think you should consider telling Chris. I don't think he'll be too sympathetic, though.'

Stephanie cupped the bowl of her glass in both hands. She was temporarily confused. She had known that Jane would be disapproving, surprised, maybe even shocked, but the coherence and simplicity of what she had experienced . . . She repeated the word silently to herself and felt it to be totally appropriate. Simplicity. That expresses it best. It was so simple, unadulterated, natural and yet unnatural.

She tried to articulate her thoughts. 'It wasn't sordid, just natural and kind of obvious, that's why it's so hard to describe . . .'

Jane shrugged. 'Just sex. Are you seeing each other again?'

Stephanie sighed and shook her head. 'I shouldn't think so. I hadn't thought about it like that. It wasn't like that.'

Jane seemed unimpressed. 'So you won't be seeing him again. But will you have sex with other people at work? When it's quiet, just before closing?'

She was smirking. Stephanie felt at once angry and misunderstood. She spoke instead of thinking, before thinking. 'Maybe this has changed me. I didn't feel immediately different, but I think that I might actually be. I knew you wouldn't approve, but I thought you'd be . . .' She tried to collect her thoughts.

Jane turned away from Stephanie and looked over her shoulder and towards the juke box. It was silent. She wondered whether she could be bothered to go over and put some money into it. It then struck her that this might in fact be a good idea, a means to walk away from the conversation, to bring about a hiatus, a gap, a space, so that when she returned they could discuss other things. She took her purse from her bag and stood up. She said, 'I'm going to put some music on the juke box.'

Stephanie didn't reply. She nodded. She watched Jane walk over

56

to the juke box and thought, 'Suddenly we have no common ground. When she comes back to the table she won't discuss this with me again. It's as though nothing can be expressed between us which will make sense, which we can both understand. When she comes back to the table she will be assured in her own mind that she is now better than me, that she has something over me, and yet . . .'

She sighed and pushed a piece of hair that had fallen across her face behind her ear. 'And yet something so incredible has happened.' She felt sad, almost bitter, but in her heart she knew that the space that had sprung up between them, the vacuum, had now opened up inside her, and it was a positive space that could be filled with so many things; ideas, possibilities. She thought, 'Words are like gifts, some people are generous and some frugal.' She decided to make herself a present by keeping quiet.

Food with Feeling

Anne Marie baked cakes every week. Usually she baked for a couple of hours every Sunday afternoon. The family had dinner at five on Sunday so she baked from two until four and then began the Meal Proper. Her husband liked her baking, he appreciated the way that she did things from scratch. Even if the results were sometimes inadequate, he still complimented her roundly and fully on effort and commitment. 'After all,' he'd say, 'this is the Take-Away Age. You do well to stand up against it with its additives and its preservatives and its factory-plastic tastes.'

Anne Marie valued his opinion. Often his family visited on a Sunday so she'd make dinner for five; for Steve, his mum, his dad, little Fiona and herself. Now she had another hungry mouth to feed on its way too; a tiny thumb-sized foetus nestled in her stomach somewhere, eating, growing and forming.

Little Fiona was almost three. Anne Marie had decided to have her children later rather than sooner. She had worked as a legal secretary for twelve years before even considering the idea of conception, pregnancy and birth. Fiona had burst into the world when Anne Marie was already in her thirty-fourth year of life, although she and Steve had been married for ever.

She had begun baking just before Fiona was born because she thought that it made the home more homely and she and Steve more of a proper family. She needn't have worried though because he took to being a father like a duck to water. He leapt in with his eyes closed and a finger and thumb placed firmly over his nostrils. He said that he was happy about the second baby but that he missed her extra wage coming in. He had calculated that her wage would be back in the kitty when Fiona had started at nursery school. It didn't look that way now. 'Still,' he said, 'I'm perfectly happy about the new baby, and at least we don't have to buy a new pram this time.'

Steve worked in his father's business, which was a small concern that produced paper cups and plates for children's parties, featuring popular cartoon characters. The business barely supported two executive wages so Steve had to work extra hard for less than you'd expect. He had his eye on the long term. His dad took a back seat, spending long lunch-hours in the Hammer and Tongs, reading the *Financial Times* and smoking Lite cigars.

At the factory the workforce consisted mainly of women working part-time for under the minimum wage. They also had a couple of YOP schemes on the go. The kids learned how to stack packets of cups and plates into groups of twelve before putting them into boxes. It was illuminating work.

Anne Marie took an active interest in Steve's activities and firmly believed that he was more intelligent than her. He often hinted as much with wry smiles and gentle pats on her head whenever she made as if to discuss anything of worth. He was clever enough in his own way though, clever enough to employ attractive young women at work and to touch their hair and brush himself against them when distributing their wage packets on a Friday afternoon. The women came into his office one by one. He was like an enormous prickly hairbrush, stroking and tweaking, smoothing and glossing. At work the women secretly called him 'The Brush'. He was so obvious.

Anne Marie didn't ever like to think bad things about him, she felt that such thoughts were a kind of disloyalty, so she baked and cleaned and made as if to be a model housewife, which she was.

In many ways she led a successful life. Sundays were her days. Steve always said, 'Anne Marie, Sundays are your days, I'll read the paper. Would you mind making me a coffee before you start dinner?' Little Fiona stood on a chair at the sink and pretended to help with the washing up.

Steve's mother liked coming to their house on a Sunday because it saved her the effort of cooking. She was always on a diet, so cooking was a trial. She picked at her food. Steve always said that you could tell what sort of person someone was by the way that they ate. Of course, he'd always had a healthy appetite.

Anne Marie thought that she should enjoy baking so she tried to pretend to herself that she did. During the week she pretended to look forward to Sunday. She pretended to enjoy the planning that she assiduously put into play every Saturday morning at Asda over the meat counter and when choosing what kind of potato was best.

In fact she hated it. She hated the hot kitchen and the fiddly preparation, the peeling and primping. She hated cooking. But there was another baby on the way (of course she wanted it), another mouth to feed. She didn't want to be disloyal.

The food had begun to express her. Since the new baby had been conceived – he had been drunk, she had been drunk but purposeful – the food had begun to develop its expressive faculties to the full, especially on a Sunday when it seemed to revel in its significance. Peas and potatoes, steaks and salads all had something to say, something piquant and niggly. But dinner tasted good just the same.

Little Fiona noticed first. One week she said, 'Mummy, this lemon meringue pie seems to be angry. It tastes very bitter and the frosty bit is too sugary and full of air.'

Grandad blew smoke rings at her and said that she was a smart girl. He said, 'The whole point of this kind of dish is its contrasts; sweet and sour, creaminess and fluffiness. In many ways this pie is like a fine woman.'

Little Fiona stared at him with beguiling eyes and said, 'No, it's not just like anybody, it's like Mummy. That's what I'm saying. It's like her.'

Anne Marie asked if anyone fancied brie with biscuits and before the plates had been taken away the entire incident was forgotten.

But from then on every dish was like a person or an emotion. One week the meal was like Steve's mother. Her meal was a dish of ribs. They were lean but juicy and the sauce was menopausal. Another week the meal was like Steve. They had pheasant and the meat was dark and rich. It was too much. The vegetables were in riot against the game, they hung about in clusters and moved contemptuously around the plate. Anne Marie had made a strong gravy to swamp the meal's strength. It disguised almost everything.

Sometimes her meals expressed people that they didn't even

know. When the Minister for Social Security didn't increase Child Benefit, Anne Marie produced an incredible risotto that expressed him to perfection. When *Brookside* was going through an especially engaging period, when the story was particularly exciting and realistic, she produced a series of meals that expressed the programme's leading characters and their dilemmas. Barry Grant was encapsulated in a daring toad-in-the-hole. 'Not a proper Sunday meal,' Steve said, 'but enjoyable just the same.'

Since little Fiona's first comments on the subject, Anne Marie had become increasingly aware of her random compulsion to produce food with feeling. Her meals were like feelings; sweet, sharp, painful, joyous, confused, jumbled. Her tarts were like tears, her swiss rolls just didn't understand.

Anne Marie thought it all through. She was now five months pregnant. She thought it through and decided that maybe the meals were to do with the baby. Maybe the meals were the baby's introduction to the emotions. She felt like the baby knew everything about everyone and everything about everything. Inside her the baby felt smug. But she was none the wiser herself. When she cooked on a Sunday she felt a pulling from deep inside her stomach, it was as though the baby's movements were hunger pains. It was like the baby was saying, 'Make me real, make a meal that is me, then I will become a proper person. Give me feelings and a soul.' But every time Anne Marie tried to bake something that expressed the baby she made something or someone else. One week she came close. She thought she'd done it when she baked some coconut cookies but when little Fiona saw them she shouted, 'Look Mummy, it's me! They smell so young and nice.'

Steve said that the coconut got stuck in his teeth. He picked at it. He found it irritating.

Anne Marie worried for her new baby. She wondered what she should do for it. Steve was complaining of indigestion all the time. He moaned. She thought, 'God, he never says what he really feels, he never truly expresses himself to me.'

But she couldn't gauge her own feelings either. She could only bake and cook. She hated doing it. She thought, 'Feelings are such dirty and confusing things. I wish I understood them.' Something big had to happen. Something more.

When Anne Marie was eight months pregnant with a huge stomach and swollen ankles something big finally did happen. Over the past weeks she had baked Cilla Black, her milkman, Roger Scruton, the Famous Mr Ed, Sarah Bernhardt, Michael Aspel and the girl on the cold meats counter in Tesco's. The larger she grew the more Steve complained about how he missed her wage. Every Sunday afternoon in front of the television when his parents had finally gone home he'd say, 'Of course I'm glad about the baby, it's just that we miss your money in the kitty. I'm not made of money myself and times are hard.' On these occasions the baby's tiny hands punched and pulled inside her. She felt as though everything was disguised, as though she didn't have the power to see anything as it really was.

The following Sunday she started baking especially early. She started to make a cake, a big three-layered coffee-and-walnut gâteau. She had never made a gâteau before so it was something of a random operation. No single recipe seemed adequate so she combined three different ones. The cake was a real original. As she cooked, the baby pulled inside her and she thought, 'Maybe this is it. Maybe this cake is going to be the baby.' This thought excited her because the cake was so rich and special and extravagant.

Steve came into the kitchen for a moment as she prepared the cake and moaned that the ingredients were too lavish. He said, 'What's wrong with a plain madeira or a Victoria sponge?' Anne Marie couldn't explain what was wrong with them. She was unable to articulate.

The gâteau took three hours and thirty-five minutes to complete. It was incredible. When she had finished it Anne Marie felt totally fulfilled and serene. Unfortunately she only had enough time left to make a perfunctory meal of chops and salad for Sunday dinner. Steve grimaced when it was served. His mum said something about it being good for her diet. The meal didn't express anything. The food was just food and it went down easily. Little Fiona looked vaguely disappointed as the plates were cleared away, but her face lit up when her mum brought forth the gâteau with a nervous show of self-conscious ceremony. She brought it out as if to say. 'This is my new child, please don't find fault with him.'

Everyone stared at the gâteau. Its chocolate and coffee decorations glimmered. Anne Marie took a knife to it with the slightest of winces as she cut out four large slices. They began to eat. She couldn't bear to touch it herself even though the baby stormed inside her like a tiny hurricane.

Little Fiona took a mouthful and said, 'I love you, Mummy. I hope I have a little baby brother to play with and that you won't love him more than me.'

Steve's dad collected some crumbs of walnut sponge together with his fingers and thrust them into his mouth as he said, 'My wife never cooks properly for me. My son's a real opportunist. He makes the most of every opportunity; at home, at work, with the girls in the factory. I suppose you don't even know it. I wonder what sort of a father he'll make this time around. He has his eye on the long term, on the main chance.'

Steve's mum licked some cream from the corner of her mouth and said, 'He says I never cook. Why the hell should I when I have to starve myself all the time to remain unnaturally thin so that he'll look at me every once in a while. The kids ruined my figure, I've always resented them for that. They'll ruin yours if you're not careful, Anne Marie. You look such a frump already and you're only thirty-seven. No wonder Steve plays the field.'

Anne Marie stood by the table and clasped her hands over her stomach as though she had a bad, bad cramp. She thought, 'Is this cake the baby? Is this what I've made?'

Then little Fiona said, 'Mummy, may I have some more of the Truth Cake? I like it even though it hurts a bit. It made me feel so light. May I have some more?'

Steve cut into the cake roughly and pulled out another slice for Fiona. He then said, 'I don't want another baby, Anne Marie, I don't need these complications. When Dad dies I'll own the company and I'll be able to do as I please. I'm sick of your cookery, I'm sick of it and yet it's the only thing about you that's worthwhile. You're so careful and slow it makes me laugh. I don't know when it was that I started to find you so ridiculous, maybe I always did. Whatever happens, just keep the new baby out of my hair, that's all I ask. Just keep it out of my way.'

Anne Marie watched everyone finish their slices and then cleared away the plates in silence. She took the cake to the kitchen and placed it on the sideboard. Almost half was left. She stared at it blankly and felt engulfed by a great wave of depression and confusion. She thought, 'Why did I make this? I thought that I was expressing the new baby, but all I did was to bake a Hate-Cake.'

Inside her was a smooth stroking feeling as though the baby was rocking and soothing her. She touched her stomach. From within her something called. It said, 'This isn't hatred, it's the truth. This is what feelings hide and show, disguise and reveal. Have some, have some.' She thought, 'Maybe the baby is the truth. I feel as though he is finally real, as though he made all of this happen. I wanted the baby because I wanted to find out the truth about everything.'

She removed her hand from her stomach and cut into the cake. Then she ate one slice, another slice and then a third slice.

She swallowed her final mouthful and suddenly felt as though a light was shining from behind her eyes. In her stomach the new child was laughing. She brushed her hair back in one smooth movement and walked towards the open door. Everyone sat around the dining table in silence. They turned towards her. She stood in the doorway and smiled. Then she said, 'I want to tell you the truth, and the truth hurts.'

Symbiosis: Class Cestoda

The first thing they did after saying hello was to move straight into Shelly's bedroom and have sex. They had been voluntarily apart for five months. During this entire period Sean had seen Shelly on only one single occasion, and that had been at Sainsbury's where he had been trying to get hold of some Turkish Delight for his mother. He had seen her by the bread counter buying a French stick. She was chatting to the young girl who was serving her. He couldn't imagine what about. His first impulse was to think, 'She's lost so much weight, she seems so cheerful', as an afterthought, 'without me'. His second impulse was to duck behind a stack of soup tins as she turned in his direction and then to scurry away when he was sure that she would not notice him. He didn't want to see her, to speak to her, but equally he didn't want her to see him making a quick getaway. That would hardly seem dignified for either party.

He was twenty-seven and she was twenty-five. They had been 'seeing' each other for four years and for the last two of those four years they had been living together. She rented a flat in Wood Green close to the tube station. He had opted to move in with her and initially things had been fine.

She had never been thin. She was what most dietitians would call pear-shaped, but she was five feet and eight inches tall, which is a good size for a woman, and that height somehow undermined the size of her hips and made her shape seem less obvious. Unfortunately, within a year of their practical union she had begun to gain weight.

Sean knew that he was hardly the perfect partner, that his idea of faithful was to try and think of her when he was screwing other women. But he firmly believed that in other respects he was an excellent mate. He helped with the housework, he bought her flowers, he told her that she was beautiful.

It would be a lie to say that when she gained weight he didn't find her any less attractive. Her eating was perpetual and compulsive. Invariably she had something in her mouth; if not part of a jam tart or a sausage roll then some chewing gum or a boiled sweet. Sometimes he felt that her eating was a way of distancing herself from him; as though the layers of fat were an attempt to keep him away. Even so, she was always saying that she loved him, always saying that she needed him.

Her doctor had recommended a trial separation, a cooling-off period so that they could both analyse their feelings at a sensible distance. By this time she was well over fourteen stone and what the medical profession might describe as clinically depressed. He had been more than willing to accept this new development in their relationship. His mother had clucked her tongue at him when he had arrived home again with a suitcase and several carrier bags, and had told him that he just wasn't willing to stick things out, to sort things out.

Shelly had a theory about something called Symbiosis. She had learned about this word at school in her biology lessons. It had always been a word with great significance and relevance to her life. She loved the feel of the word in her mouth as she said it out loud. She thought, 'Everyone has words that are particular to them, that are significant to them, and this word, this idea is the most important factor in my life.'

She dreamed a lot about love. She wanted to be in a situation in the future where she could literally not survive without the love, kindness and care of a man and he, similarly, would feel the same way about her. Symbiosis (*sim-bi-ō'sis*) n. *the living together of two kinds of organisms to their mutual advantage.*

Shelly believed that men were altogether a different kind of organism to women. She had tried to make things work out with Sean but he had wanted everything his own way. He still told her that he found her attractive, but he also still told her that he found other women attractive too. After sex he would regularly disappear off into the bathroom with a girlie magazine and she would lie alone in bed and try to think of something else. She didn't say anything because she wanted it to work out, she wanted him to need her and she knew that she needed him, someone, something, anyone, him.

She hated dieting so much. Since early puberty she had been on diets of one kind or another. After a while it became clear to her that her metabolism was so slow that eating a peanut added several inches to her hips, thighs and stomach. Her relationship with food, with that which could be consumed, was passionate, impetuous, exotic, erotic. She loved eating, she loved to swallow, she loved to taste sweetness on her tongue and in her mouth. She would happily have given a month of her life for a mouthful of sherbet or a meaty rib in bar-BQ sauce.

When Sean proved too much for her she didn't sulk or argue, instead she ate, and the food appeared palpably on her body, each meal became a dimple in her thigh or a part of the warm tyre around her waist.

Underneath all the bullshit she knew that the weight was also her way of trying to make Sean find her less physically attractive. She wanted him to need her for herself, she wanted security. Instead he would stare at her as she lay in the bath or as she tried to get dressed and undressed and he would say, 'You've put on so much weight lately that when we make love it's like fucking a barrel of lard.' Invariably as an afterthought he'd add, 'It's a good job that I like barrels of lard.'

She'd try to smile.

A lot can happen in five months. The first thing they did after saying hello was to move into Shelly's bedroom and have sex. After sex Shelly got up immediately and went to the bathroom. She had a wash and then came back into the bedroom and started to get dressed.

Sean lay in bed and watched her. He said, 'I've really missed you.' It was almost true; he was sick of living at home and her flat was convenient and she cooked well and he didn't have to try so hard with her as he did with other women.

She smiled as she hooked up her bra and adjusted the material over her breasts. She said, 'I suppose I've missed you.'

He said, 'Why are you getting dressed?'

She grinned. 'I thought you could take me out to dinner. I fancy an Italian or a Chinese.'

He sat up straight in bed and surveyed her thoroughly. Then he said, 'You're looking great, Shelly, do you know that? You've lost a load of weight and it really suits you.'

She nodded, 'I know.'

He was surprised by this new confidence, this calm assurance. In five months she seemed to have changed incalculably. He felt rather piqued by this but also attracted. She seemed so happy.

Suddenly it struck him that she was seeing another man; there was something about her that was so serene and fulfilled. The idea of her with another man made his stomach churn. He said, 'Have you been seeing someone else?'

She laughed. 'Why?'

She was pulling on some jeans which five months ago wouldn't have gone beyond her knees. He shrugged. 'I dunno. You seem different. You've lost weight. Before you'd have never got dressed like this, straight away.'

She went into the bathroom to fix her make-up and brush her hair. As she left the bedroom she looked over her shoulder and said, 'Let's go and eat, Sean, I'm starving.'

In the end they chose Chinese. On their way to the restaurant – along the High Road, next to the Shopping City – Sean noticed how other men stared at Shelly as she walked. She seemed aloof and oblivious. He wanted to hold her hand as they strolled along but she held her handbag in the hand closest to him which made this difficult.

They chatted about work and Shelly asked how his mum was. He said she was fine. It all felt rather odd and unnatural. He had imagined that she would be tense when she saw him but in fact she seemed perfectly relaxed and at her ease. If anything he was the one who felt uncomfortable. His previous role in their relationship had been one of indispensability. The whole point of him had been the fact that she needed him. He knew that she needed someone. He felt nosy and jealous but he said nothing until they were seated at a table in the restaurant.

The waiter flirted with Shelly as they ordered their meal. He noticed their eye contact and it made his stomach contract. After the waiter had left their table with the order (Shelly was hungry and had ordered a substantial meal), he played with his cutlery, making his finger into a flat, straight scale and trying to balance his knife on the finger so that it didn't tip off, then his fork, then his spoon. Shelly watched him with a half smile flickering around the corners of her lips.

Eventually he said, 'Is there someone else?'

She shrugged. 'I don't have another man in my life at the moment, Sean, no. That was part of the deal, remember? It was a trial separation but our view in the short term was to getting back together.'

He nodded. 'I know that, it's just that you seem so different. You're a different person to the girl I left five months back. You seem above it all now, like someone in love.'

Secretly he wondered if she was just in love with him and he had never really noticed before, had never really seen her before tonight. She shook her head. 'I've already told you that I'm not in love, I'm just happy. If I'm in love with anything then it's food.'

He frowned. 'What do you mean?'

His voice was rough and unsympathetic. She smiled at this roughness. 'I mean that I'm happy because I'm using new sources in my life to find satisfaction and contentment. For some people it's drink, for others it's sex, for others it's drugs. Well for me it's food. Eating makes me happy. Before I thought that I only ate because I was unlucky in love but now I know that I eat because I like it.'

He had never been able to understand her delight in large spoonfuls of raspberry and rum mousse, the condensed glee in a packet of plain chocolate digestives. He said, 'The doctor told you that compulsive behaviour always leads to unhappiness.'

She smirked. 'Fuck the doctor.'

He frowned. 'Are you?'

She laughed. 'Be serious Sean!'

He smiled, but it was the smile of someone who thinks that they understand something when really they understand nothing. She said, 'Compulsive behaviour is to a large extent something that people rely upon to get out of bed in the morning. It's what makes the world go around.'

He shook his head. 'No, that's habit. If something is compulsive it's usually bad for you.'

She smiled at him icily. 'Like sex?'

He smiled back. 'That's pleasure.'

The waiter arrived at the table with the starters, some spring rolls and prawn crackers. Shelly ate a couple of the crackers and then started on a spring roll. He looked down at his plate but didn't feel hungry. She said, 'The more I indulge my compulsions, the less I feel them ruling my life. It's weird. You'd think it would be the other way around but it isn't. Eat up, it's delicious.'

He tried a mouthful and it did taste good.

Her voracious appetite, which had developed two or three years into their relationship, had always violently irritated him. When they had first started going out she ate virtually nothing. When they went to restaurants he would joke about how little she ate as she ordered the salad option and ate very slowly, chewing each mouthful with great restraint and discipline. He thought it appropriate that women should behave this way; women who gained too much enjoyment from food, greedy women, were usually too demanding in bed. They made him nervous.

He stared nervously at Shelly as she chewed and swallowed with great finesse and rapidity. After several minutes the waiter came to take their plates away. Sean had left most of his starter but Shelly's plate was clean.

The waiter smiled at her as he took her plate. 'You enjoyed that?' Shelly nodded. 'It was delicious, but don't worry, I've still got room for the main course.'

The waiter pulled a face which implied that he found it hard to believe that someone who looked as good as Shelly didn't have to starve themselves to keep in trim. Sean was sure that he was staring at her breasts. He nodded curtly and dismissed the waiter with a brisk thank you.

Shelly touched her napkin to both corners of her mouth. She looked around her and studied the other people in the restaurant. Sean stared at her face; her green eyes, her strong nose, her dark black eyebrows and her curling fringe. He said, 'Your hair suits you in that short bob style.'

She dragged her eyes from the couple sitting by the door and focused them dreamily on Sean's face. 'Does it?'

She paused and then before he could answer said, 'Yes, I think it does. It's still too curly. Bobs should be very straight ideally.'

He nodded in silence, pretending that he understood or cared. She reached out one of her hands and caught a droplet of wax that was dripping down the small white candle in the centre of the table on the side of her middle finger. It felt hot on her hand for a second and then solidified. She began to draw her hand back again but before she could properly do so Sean put out his hand and took hold of hers. Their arms were suspended uncomfortably in mid-air. She squeezed his hand fondly and then drew hers away.

The waiter brought the main course. As he dished up his portions Sean said, 'What's going to happen now, between us?'

In his car on his way around to her flat he had imagined this situation but the roles had been reversed. He had visualized Shelly, all tearful and cloying, biting her lip, begging him to come back to her. She'd change, she'd be less possessive, anything.

Shelly didn't answer his question immediately. He repeated himself: 'What's going to happen now, Shelly?'

She frowned and eventually said, 'I don't know.'

She started eating. She had chicken chow mein with mixed vegetables in soy sauce. It tasted heavenly. Sean couldn't eat. Everything seemed to be going wrong. He knew that Shelly needed him, needed someone. He put down his knife and fork and said, 'Shelly, please tell me if there's someone else.'

She didn't reply. He began to feel jealous and angry, bitter. After a

73

few minutes watching her eat he said, 'I bet you'll regret this meal tomorrow. It'll take it's toll on your figure.'

Shelly stopped chewing and looked into his eyes. 'I shouldn't think so.'

He frowned. 'How come?'

She finished her mouthful and curled some more chow mein on to her fork, 'I don't gain weight any more. It's connected to something called symbiosis.'

He grimaced. 'What's that supposed to mean?'

'It means that I don't gain weight any more but I can eat what I like.'

The flame on the candle flickered for a moment as the door of the restaurant opened. His eyes focused on the flame for a second, then returned to her face. 'How is that possible?'

She sighed and put down her knife and fork and then leaned forward on her elbows and whispered, 'I've got a tapeworm.'

He wasn't sure that he'd heard her correctly. 'What?'

She smiled as though what she was telling him caused her infinite joy. 'I've got a tapeworm, Sean, it's symbiosis. We both depend on each other to carry on.'

Sean shook his head in disbelief. 'What do you mean, Shelly? Is this a joke or something?'

Worms disgusted him. He had seen part of a nature programme on television a few weeks before which had featured something about worms that had made him almost physically sick. He had turned it over straight away.

Shelly returned to her meal, unperturbed. After a mouthful she said, 'I got him by eating raw mincemeat. It took a while and obviously I had to specify certain parts of the animal, you know, stomach, offal. I actually told the butcher that I wanted meat minced for my dog. As I said though, it took several attempts.'

Sean's lip curled in disgust. 'You ate raw dog meat?'

She shook her head. 'No, low quality meat, not from a can. Lots of animals get tapeworms. Obviously though there are many different varieties. It's very complicated because I think they reproduce in lots of different ways. I went to great lengths to get mine.'

Sean still couldn't be sure that Shelly wasn't joking. He said, 'What do you call it? Trevor?'

She laughed. It was the first time that she had laughed properly all evening. 'I don't have a formal name for him – I think he's asexual. I haven't read all that much about them.'

The waiter returned to the table to make sure that their meal was all right. Shelly answered, smiling, 'It's absolutely delicious, thank you.' Sean just continued to stare at her face. Once the waiter had moved away he picked up his fork and tried to eat one of the lightly battered prawn balls on his plate. As he chewed Shelly said, 'You see, the tapeworm consumes my undigested food so that it doesn't have the chance to turn into fat. That's my theory anyway. He then uses the food to grow and reproduce himself. He sort of develops another segment which divides away from his body after a certain period. This segment, I'm slightly confused on this point though, this segment then either stays in the stomach, hooking on to a prime place, or it's flushed out with your body fluids.'

Sean said nothing. He was pushing prawn and batter around his mouth but he couldn't swallow. Shelly took this silence as an indication of interest so she added, 'I'm glad you're not a biologist, Sean, because I'm explaining this very badly.'

Sean carried on chewing. On his forehead were slight beads of perspiration. He picked up his napkin and blotted them. Shelly took a sip of wine and said, 'I have to be careful about alcohol. I sometimes think that it must be bad for him so I don't drink very much any more. That's something else good that he's brought to my life.'

Sean pushed his mouthful of well-chewed food into his cheek and said, 'What happens when it grows, Shelly?'

She shrugged and picked up her knife and fork again, 'I'm not absolutely sure. In general I think they just get bigger and bigger until they fill up all your tubes. I think they can grow to an enormous size. They just grow bigger and bigger and reproduce.'

Sean shuddered. 'And what happens then? I'm sure they're harmful.'

Suddenly an image flashed into his mind, an image that he had seen accompanied by the voice of David Attenborough. There had been a snail on a leaf. As it ate the leaf it had consumed some sort of worm the size of a pin head. The worm lived and grew inside the snail, created a home for itself in this new snail-stomach world. After several weeks the maggot had grown rather large. It became visible inside one of the snail's two feelers. It grew and grew until eventually it filled the feeler entirely. After a while it looked as though, instead of a feeler sticking out of the snail's head, it had a large, independent, squirming maggot whose movements were curtailed only by a thin layer of the snail's translucent skin. The maggot moved, squelched, writhed under the snail's skin, eating, growing.

Several days later the snail's other feeler began to fatten up, to grow pale, to move against its own will as another maggot appeared in this feeler. Sean hadn't been able to tell whether this was the same maggot or a different one. They certainly looked like two fully formed and independent creatures. Eventually the snail had no feelers left, just two white maggots sticking out of the top of its head, living on its juices, eating it while it carried on moving and living and breathing. The maggots shuddered and vibrated inside the snail's feelers, its eyes, prisoners in its skin, eating him.

Sean had yelped his horror and had snatched for the remote control to switch it off. He couldn't stop thinking about it afterwards though. He was sure that the snail must've died, but after how long? He felt like gagging.

Shelly had almost completed her meal. She was saying, 'Sean, eat something. It's such a waste.'

He spat out his masticated mouthful into a napkin. She said, 'I haven't been so happy in a long time, Sean. The only tiny way that I notice the worm is when I go to the toilet. Often when I go now a segment of the worm comes out in my urine.'

One of Sean's main rules of love was that women didn't go to the toilet; or if they went they did different things there than men. He refused to have his idealism shattered. Shelly had always been very circumspect about her personal habits in the past. She had always called the toilet the Little Girls' Room. When she said it he liked to imagine that women kept dolls and horses and perfume and lipstick in the Little Girls' Room, that they popped in there for a bit of fun and then came out again, beautiful, perfect and squeaky clean. He was a firm believer in the use of feminine deodorants.

Shelly was saying, 'I think the segment is just part of the worm that is dead because when I've studied it it doesn't move or anything. It's not like an independent life form . . .'

Sean couldn't believe that Shelly was saying these things; he interrupted, 'This is all a tiny bit intimate, Shelly.'

She shrugged, 'I don't know. I think I've really changed in that respect over the past few months. I used to be embarrassed about my body before and the things that it does naturally. My tapeworm has changed all that. It's like I'm now involved in a very natural and obvious relationship. It's like I can see at last how I relate to the world as a creature; to trees and grass and cows and pigs, and the moon's cycles and the sea. We all are alive in a similar way. It's all connected and we all depend on each other, in a sort of chain of existence.'

As she spoke the waiter returned to their table and took away their plates. Shelly smiled at him as he completed this task and said, 'I'd love an Irish coffee.'

He nodded and looked at Sean. Sean said, 'Just a plain coffee for me, please.'

Shelly straightened the table cloth and picked up a few crumbs to put in the ashtray. Sean felt inside his jacket pocket and took out a couple of cigarettes. He offered Shelly one. She shook her head. 'I've given up.' He raised his eyebrows then stuck a cigarette in his mouth and lit it. After inhaling he said, 'Shelly, you've got to get rid of that worm.'

She smiled. 'No.'

He exhaled vigorously. 'Well, what's going to happen when it grows to an enormous size? I'm sure you eat enough to treble its size every other day.'

She ignored this insult and said, 'I'm going to keep this one for ten months then get rid of it. Afterwards I'll get another small one and start from scratch all over again. That means it'll never get out of control.'

The waiter brought them their coffees. Shelly thanked him and took a sip of the hot, sweet, creamy liquid. Sean was momentarily quiet so she said, 'I'm going to have to read up on the whole thing because I'm not one hundred per cent sure how they reproduce. If the little segments that come out in my urine are baby worms then maybe I'll have to try and swallow one of those.' She paused and then added, 'They aren't very big but they've got hooks on them. When I pee they hang on to the lip of my body with their hooks and I have to unhook them myself. It's quite simple when you know how.'

Sean's expression was full of an incredulous horror. She smiled. 'It's all right, Sean, it doesn't hurt and it doesn't bother me.'

Sean's mind was now turning over very rapidly. He was thinking of the sex they had indulged in an hour or so before. He couldn't stop himself; he said, 'I couldn't have caught one earlier, could I?'

She frowned. 'I shouldn't think so.'

Then she smiled. 'I think you would've seen it if it had hooked on to the end of your prick.' She started to laugh. 'Imagine if the entire worm had hooked itself on, all eleven or twelve inches of it. You'd have become rather confused when you went to the bathroom!'

She spluttered with laughter as she sipped her coffee.

Sean was stony-faced. He said, 'You don't give a shit about me any more, do you? About my feelings in all of this?'

She stopped laughing and shrugged. 'You've never given a shit about me in the past, Sean. In fact I think that I can honestly say that I have had more help and support from my tapeworm over the past five months than you have given me in the last four years.' As she said this she tapped her stomach with her left hand and then took a swig of her Irish coffee.

Sean didn't know whether he wanted to live with her any more, whether he loved her, but he was damn sure that he wasn't going to be compared to her tapeworm and come out of this comparison at a disadvantage. He said, 'That thing is eating you up inside. It's a parasite.'

She nodded. 'Yes it is, and the two of you have a whole lot in common. Unfortunately, you didn't improve my self-image like this tapeworm has. It needs me. You never needed me. It's helped me. You never helped me.'

She finished her coffee and he stubbed out his cigarette. She started to put her jacket on. 'I've got a new direction in my life now, Sean. I've learned that I can survive without you, that I can be attractive and desirable and funny and interesting without needing to have you around to tell me what I am or what I can be.'

He shook his head. 'You've got a real problem, Shelly.'

She stood up. 'No, you have, Sean. I'm leaving now and you can pay the bill.'

As she left the restaurant she winked at the waiter.

The Afghan War

Anthony Bland stared at the assembled company with his rather murky, pink-tinged, morose eyes and said miserably, 'I've put on two stone since the split. Sarah always used to call this part of me' – he patted his significant gut with tender regretfulness – 'her waistline. She'd say, "Anthony, it's my waistline too. I've fought to keep you in trim. I feel as though I own that part of your body. I've looked after it for so long."' He shuddered, and then sniffed mournfully.

Hetty Thompson unconsciously tensed her buttocks and pushed her hips forward. This small gesture had been adapted into her day-to-day life by her Holistix teacher, who said that it helped to mould the body into a more beautiful shape. Now she did it, almost without thought, whenever she was forced to stand still for more than thirty or forty seconds; in shopping queues, doing the washing-up, cutting up vegetables in the kitchen. As she made this tiny gesture she said to Anthony, 'We're sick of this, Ant.' (Most of Sarah's friends abbreviated Anthony's name to 'Ant'. He had secretly always hated it. It made him feel as though they simply couldn't be bothered to expend more than half a lungful of air on pronouncing his name, as though he just wasn't important enough.) She continued, 'We know that this is none of our business, but the four of us couldn't bear to stand back and let this farce continue any longer. Please Ant, you're only managing to hurt yourself. It isn't dignified.'

As she finished speaking she glanced over at her husband, who was standing to her right looking rather stern. He nodded. 'Hetty's right, Ant. You've got to get on with your own life. Sarah's behaved badly, but so have you. Life is full of difficult situations and terrible decisions. We've all had our share of them . . .'

Anthony was sitting uncomfortably on a small apricot chaise longue. He wasn't lying on it, but was perched upright, both feet on the floor, at the leg end. The colour of the room – a paler apricot to the furniture – reflected on to his face and made his pasty features look like an expensive almond tart from Selfridges Food Hall. His face seemed round and sticky, slightly grainy.

He shook his head and pinched the bridge of his nose with a large pale finger and thumb. When he spoke, his voice sounded muffled. 'I suppose you've all come to get Silver.'

Nobody replied. He sighed. 'He's in the kitchen.'

The four visitors exchanged significant glances and then turned towards the doorway. Hetty said quietly, 'This is for the best, Ant. You know it makes sense.'

Anthony could feel a warm tickling in his nose, a now familiar sensation which felt like tears were being wept inside his brain, hot, internal tears which were searching frantically for all available exit routes. He knew it would end in ugliness.

He listened as the small group walked without speaking down the hallway and towards the kitchen door. When he heard the door being opened, he sprang stealthily to his feet and tip-toed after his unsuspecting predecessors in his soft leather moccasins. As he made his silent way down the hallway, he listened out for what was being said. First of all he heard Hetty's high and slightly nasal intonations saying, 'I can't see him. He must be inside his indoor kennel. Get down, Michael and have a look.' He heard Michael's stiff hip-bones clicking as he bent down on his hands and knees, then Michael's voice, 'There's a lot of hair in there. I think that's him at the back. Come on, Silver, come on!'

The group began calling and cooing and making silly kissing noises to try and encourage the dog to come out. In fact, the dog was not in the kennel at all, only a white, synthetic-fur rug.

Anthony restrained his keen impulse to peep in at them, and instead quickly slammed the door shut and turned the key, which he had furtively moved to the other side of the door at the start of their visit. He grinned to himself and rubbed his hands together.

Hetty was the first to react. Hearing the loud slamming noise and the key turning, she ran to the back door of the kitchen – which led into Anthony's very large and grand back garden – and tried to get it open. It appeared to have been effectively blockaded from the outside. Gasping with horror she turned and ran towards the door that Anthony had just locked, and tried the handle. All means of exit had been thoroughly curtailed.

Michael – still on his knees and looking slightly ridiculous – cautioned Hetty against trying the windows. He said, 'Remember, Sarah had the house windows alarmed after the break-in last summer. Let's not cause a scene, it could be embarrassing. Humour him.'

Anthony heard these words of reason and shook his head disapprovingly. As he made his way back down the hallway and towards the large white box by the front door that housed the alarm mechanism he muttered under his breath, 'Michael Pillow; always was the brains of the bunch.'

He opened the box, and felt around in his pocket for a tissue. He was a tissue man, never had time for handkerchiefs. He located a large man-sized blue tissue, slightly crumpled, and ripped it into two big pieces, then moulded them carefully and placed one piece in either ear. When he had completed this process he looked rather like a fancy fish with impressive, sprouty, decorative blue gill-shields sticking out on either side of his head. After finishing this task, he reached into the box and set off the alarm. Despite his makeshift earplugs, the high volume of noise made him wince. Nevertheless, he closed the box and marched resolutely towards the front door.

Outside in her white Mercedes, Sarah was sitting staring keenly out of her open window. She frowned when she heard the alarm go off, then let out a furious and unladylike grunt when she saw Anthony emerging from the house, ears stoppered and tissues waving on either side of his head. As he drew closer, she locked the doors and pressed the switch to wind up her window. Anthony broke into a trot to try and impede this process, and as he increased speed his bulk shuddered like a big, bold jelly in a bag. He stuck his hand into the top of the window and then screamed as the pane of glass continued to rise and then to violently crush his fingers. This short scream caused a flicker of joy to cross Sarah's now somewhat disgruntled visage. Unfortunately, the scream also triggered the temperamental mechanism in Anthony's brain which controlled the regular flow of blood around his anatomy. This switch turned on to nose-bleed mode and the blood poured forth from Anthony's unsuspecting nostrils like a fountain of bright red ink, interspersed with the occasional darker, blacker clot.

Sarah screwed her face up fastidiously. She shouted, 'Get away from my car, Anthony. Don't bleed on my car!'

From inside the car her voice sounded round and hollow, as though it came from underwater. Anthony, his hand still caught and bruising inside Sarah's window, shook his head. The blood spun from side to side in tiny spurts like the end of a troublesome garden hose. He said, 'I didn't have these nose-bleeds before, you know. The doctor said that they are stress-related. The living-room carpet will never be the same, nor the counterpane on our bed either.'

Sarah smiled grimly. 'The counterpane on *your* bed, Anthony, not mine.'

He launched his bulk on to the front of Sarah's car (his freedom of movement somewhat restricted by his trapped hand), and rubbed his streaming nose vigorously around on the large white bonnet, bloodying it, marking it, painting it like a crazed expressionist with his nose-brush. Sarah screamed shrilly and pressed the dashboard button responsible for cleaning the front windows. Ineffective soapy jets shot skywards from the base of the windscreen and disappeared uselessly over the roof of the car. When Anthony had finished, the effect created on the bonnet was of a particularly gruesome hit and run accident.

At this moment, alerted by the alarm, the police arrived. A young-looking officer glared at Sarah and tapped in a businesslike way at the window on the passenger side. She smiled hollowly but professionally and reached over to open it. The policeman peered inside at her. 'Mrs Bland, have you violated the court order again? If so . . .' She shook her head, and her sweet blonde bob lurched around her heart-shaped face like a heavy drinker at closing time. Her face was demure, but her skin had been gravelly since adolescence. She always made-up very heavily. She said, 'I haven't been near the house.'

Anthony, at this stage, had sunk to his knees on the road next to the car, his hand still trapped. He howled, 'Officer, I want to file another assault charge. Please encourage her to free my fingers.'

Sarah obliged without being asked again. Anthony clambered to his feet and pointed melodramatically towards the house with a blood-slicked finger, 'I've rounded up some human detritus for you, officer. Pet-stealers, malcontents all.'

The police officer glanced regretfully at his watch. He'd bargained on an early lunch.

In the back garden, Silver started barking like a hound from hell.

Anthony Bland was the fortunate owner of one of Britain's première dog-food companies. Sarah Bland was a petcare and grooming specialist. Her main initial involvement with Anthony (before matrimony) was as his dog's hairdresser and chiropodist. She owned an exclusive grooming parlour in Chelsea called Paws for Thought. Her speciality was Afghans, which she bred and showed all over the country. Early on in their relationship Sarah and Anthony had developed an exceptionally fine and exclusive dog shampoo together, which was soon to be sold across the country in pet shops and large supermarket chains.

Together they had worked to make Silver's Scraps the best-selling and most desirable high-quality canine food in the western hemisphere. Silver, Anthony's Afghan, nurtured and plucked and preened and directed by Sarah (she was to publicity what wax is to a candle) was a household name, was, in fact, Sarah's bread and butter in reputation terms. Although Silver was Anthony's dog, Sarah had dedicated the six years of their marriage to cutting his toenails and brushing his hair. He was her motto, her talisman, her mascot. He was to Sarah what a tin is to a can of beans, whereas Anthony was (to all intents and purposes) what an excess of hormones are to an adolescent; intrinsic but irritating.

Sarah wanted to put Silver's great marketing paw on the label of their joint shampoo venture. She believed that Anthony's success was her success too, but Anthony (rather selfishly) had insisted on dog food exclusivity. He said, 'Silver is my dog when all is said and done, Sarah. I sometimes feel as though all this fuss and attention gets on his nerves. He's just an amateur in this game, not one of your professional pampered pets. Use one of your own dogs instead.'

Sarah was convinced that Silver loved the limelight, and that Anthony didn't care about the shampoo because the initial idea had been her own. She kept saying, 'Why won't you commit yourself properly to this project, Anthony? Everybody knows that a dog must look good both inside and out to be truly successful. Cosmetic factors are important. I need Silver's face to make a success of this, not just me, we both do. This is a joint venture after all.' Anthony would close the subject by taking Silver out for a long walk.

A firm basis of their marriage had always been competitive shows of affection towards the dog. If one of them bought him a collar from Macey's, the other would buy him a jewel-encrusted pooper-scooper. The dog became a scapegoat, and somewhere along the line, in their generous displays, they forgot what it was like to be generous towards each other; they forgot what it was like to love each other. Sarah left the matrimonial home as a gesture of defiance. She didn't return.

The Annual International Afghan Appreciation Society's Summer Ball was to take place that Saturday night. This occasion was of great significance to Sarah in career terms because she had been chosen as guest of honour and was to receive an award (rumour had it, to be presented by someone in indirect contact with the Onassis blood-line) for her services over the years to the Afghan as a breed. An in-depth photo session – 'The Silver/Sarah Story' – with *Hello* magazine was also in the offing.

She needed Silver. She needed Silver at her side to open the ceremony – they had enclosed a small dog-biscuit shaped invitation with Silver's name on it along with her own – but if she couldn't have Silver (increasingly it looked that way), then she had to ensure that Anthony didn't try and sabotage her by some ruse, as yet known only to himself. She couldn't bear the idea of him bringing Silver along to the ceremony. It would look bad, especially if he hadn't groomed him properly. For Anthony it meant nothing, but she had so much on the line.

As she left the police station Sarah swallowed back a wave of nausea. She was so desperate that she had even contemplated an attempted (and temporary) reunion during the weekend so that she might make use of Silver for the duration of the ball, but she knew that Anthony was too wise, too possessive, too paranoid. It was a big problem.

Anthony sat in the back garden brushing Silver's long, golden hair and musing silently on the turn of events. He was satisfied with his morning's work. He said out loud – the sound of his voice causing the dog to start and pull momentarily on his lead – 'I showed 'em, Silver. These professional animal care types are demons. The worst sorts. Care only for money and prestige and profit. I think I'm better than that. You've always been mine and I've always loved you, come what may.'

Suddenly a thought entered his head, a thought so intoxicating that the joy of it made him feel as though his brain was soaking in rum, floating in a sea of alcohol. He threw down the brush and ran into the house. Several minutes later he re-emerged holding a small electric razor, which was already vibrating in his hand.

Silver stared at the buzzing razor with his big grey-brown eyes and sighed despondently. He was a decent sort of animal, but lately had begun to feel rather stressed out.

As Anthony sheared away at Silver's fur, he felt warm, salty blood trickling down his throat. He remembered the tissues in his ears and pulled them out, then, without needing to remould them, pushed the ear-stoppers up either nostril. He tried to remember to breathe through his mouth.

Sarah had her spies. A particularly helpful and obliging kennel-maid in her employ was more than happy to spend her working hours – and several more hours overtime – scrutinizing the Bland residence, keeping an eye on Silver, making sure that Sarah was kept abreast of all developments.

On Friday night, Sarah was sitting somewhat gracelessly (her legs up on the desk) in the reception area of Paws for Thought. They were closed. Even allowing for the incident with Anthony earlier on, it had been a most depressing day. Countless clients had made references to the AAS ball and award ceremony. All expressed an enthusiasm to see Silver in the fur, so to speak, with his hair like a waterfall of smooth, creamy, champagne follicles.

Sarah was full of a deep, numbing, inexplicable sense of foreboding. She sensed that Anthony was up to something, was willing to go to extreme lengths to humiliate her. She stared at her knees and tried to think of something else. Instead she wondered whether cellulite and fat were the same thing, or if cellulite was something more complex that you couldn't get rid of merely by dieting. Her knees looked dimply. Anthony had always loved her dimples.

The front door of the shop crashed open and Sarah's obliging kennel-maid ran in, panting, red-faced, slightly hysterical. Sarah removed her legs from the desk and pulled down her skirt. She then strode over to the girl and, taking hold of her shoulders, shook her violently while saying, 'For God's sake, tell me what's happened, tell me what he's done, tell me!'

The girl's teeth chattered but she forced out the word 'razor'.

Sarah gasped. 'You mean, you mean he's . . .' She gulped, '. . . suicide?'

The girl shook her head and then breathed deeply to try and control her vocal chords. 'Worse than that. It's the dog. He's shaved the dog. Hasn't shaved the whole dog, though. Only its bottom.'

Sarah dropped to her knees, wrapping her arms around her head like someone shielding themselves from a bomb. After a short duration her voice emerged, wavering, muffled, 'How does it look?'

The kennel-maid sobbed and rung her hands, 'Oh Mrs Bland, it looks . . . it looks *awful!*'

Anthony stared smugly out of the kitchen window at Silver, who was trotting around the back garden, the hair on his body swinging regally. He was such a proud dog, a great specimen. Anthony thought to himself, 'I love him! Everything I've done I've done for him. He's my child. This cut is just cosmetic, peripheral, like discipline; being cruel to be kind. Let's see how Sarah reacts to it though!'

He couldn't repress a tiny chuckle as Silver turned around and brought his beautifully shaved rump into full view. Anthony's chest puffed out proudly as he perused his handiwork. It wasn't just a shaved bottom, it was more than that. Anthony had shaved a large heart shape across the dog's buttocks which spread over the entire rump area, an area that was now whitish, surprisingly skinny and amazingly unattractive. The base of the heart, its bottom 'v', found a lovely focus just under the dog's anus. Anthony had shaved the tail too, for good measure, which waved around like an obscene, pale, twig.

Silver knew that something strange had happened to his rear end. Occasionally he craned his head round and endeavoured to sniff at it. That part of his body now felt extremely vulnerable and cold. He dreaded winter, when he might be forced to perform his more basic bodily functions crouching in the snow. On such occasions, a bottom really needed hair.

Anthony turned from the window and set about making some popcorn in the microwave.

Sarah had been awake all night. Initially she had debated taking one of her other show Afghans to the ball, pretending that it was Silver. But she was well aware that everybody knew how Silver actually looked. He was the celebrity after all; people had grown accustomed to his beautiful blond hair and proud, serene gaze and gait. He was a star. Anyway, Anthony had to be taken into account. He was obviously planning to make an appearance with the real new look Silver in tow. She knew that everyone would presume that she was responsible for the cut. It didn't matter whether they found out the truth later. As a businesswoman, Sarah knew that initial impressions are the ones that really stick, the most fundamental, the longest lasting, the most suggestive.

At 5 a.m., red eyed, slightly frazzled, the big solution to her problems finally popped into her brain. It had taken its time in coming, but it was worth the wait. She let out a small, shrill, desperate scream, then sprang out of bed and threw on some clothes.

Since the split she had been living in her mother's small flat in Pimlico. She dashed downstairs, out of the building and jumped into her Mercedes. She started the engine and pointed the nose of her car in the direction of Paws for Thought and its adjacent kennels. Her fingers and hands were tickling as she pushed round the steering wheel and the gear-stick. She was ready for work. She was ready for action, ready, almost, for anything.

Saturday night. Anthony was waiting outside the large reception hall for the AAS Ball in his station wagon. Silver was sat in the back, his twiggy tail stuck miserably between his back legs. He was a sensitive dog who often felt things too deeply. Sarah had used to say – maybe she still said it, but his doggy ears never heard it now – that 'Silver's soul is just too great. He has too great a soul, at least too great a soul for an Afghan.'

Silver was burdened, felt a sensation of weight and dread in his heart which perfectly complimented the sensation of light airiness around his buttocks.

Anthony squinted out of the window and towards the well-lit entrance. Several photographers were hanging about on the steps, waiting for scoops (not of the pooper variety), waiting for guests of honour, important people and important dogs. Anthony finished his packet of ready-salted Hula-Hoops and, after screwing up the packet and throwing it carelessly out of the window, glanced down at his wrist watch. He turned and peered over his shoulder at Silver, saying, 'Won't be long now, gorgeous,' and adjusted his shirt and bow tie.

A sudden commotion to the right of the hall indicated the arrival of the guest of honour. Sarah arrived, surrounded by people, the flashing lights of photographers, shouts, whistles, a surprising volume of noise, interspersed with the odd, occasional, hysterical doggy bark.

Anthony peered across the road, trying to see what she was

wearing, what she was doing, but he could only see the top of her blonde bob as she climbed the stairs into the hall and disappeared from sight.

He waited for five minutes, gauging the tickle at the top of his nose, a dangerous, familiar tickle, waiting for a warm trickle of blood, but none came. After the five minutes were up, he opened the car door, climbed out and then opened the back door for Silver. Silver clambered out and waited patiently for his collar and lead to be adjusted. He felt full of a supernatural doggy dread. The evening air felt cold and treacherous.

Anthony sniffed noisily and then made his way towards the brightly lit entrance. Silver followed, dragging his paws, slinking, head hanging.

The hall was packed, brightly lit, full of yells, whistles and a strange, unexpected, buoyant hysteria. Anthony frowned. He had expected this kind of atmosphere after his appearance with the new-look Silver in tow, but not before. As he entered the main hall itself and began to walk up the long, red-carpeted aisle towards the main stage, he squinted short-sightedly forwards to try and see what was happening.

He caught sight of Sarah's head, her yellow hair. She was wearing a beautiful, white-sequinned dress, a plain, close-fitting dress which made her look – Anthony couldn't deny it, even to himself – which made her look almost angelic. She glowed.

At the end of three matching white-sequinned leads were three of her best show Afghans from the kennels, all nice dogs, Anthony thought, but not of Silver's calibre.

He drew closer. The crowd – at last – were beginning to notice him: he sensed a wave of developing interest and enthusiasm generated by his sudden appearance. Now he was within ten or so steps of the stage. Sarah was saying, 'Thanks to you all, ladies and gentlemen, but most of all, thanks to the dogs that have made all this possible.'

She turned, twirled, span around to face the rear of the stage. The dogs turned with her. The audience screamed in unison.

Each of the dogs had been shaved, shaved in the same way as

Silver. Their three heart-shaped blueish patches shone under the bright stage lights. The first dog had a large letter 'I' on its bottom, the second the word 'Love', the third the word 'Afghans'.

The crowd cooed and then cheered. The three dogs waved their tails in unison. Then Anthony noticed Sarah's bottom. Her own white-sequinned and well-shaped tush had been decorated too, not shaven, but covered in a big Afghan-hair heart which swished and swirled as she hitched and rolled her hips Monroesquely.

Anthony gazed, aghast. Sarah half-turned, caught his eye and said, 'Anthony has brought Silver, ladies and gentlemen. Our very special guest of honour!'

The audience applauded. Anthony could do nothing but climb up on to the stage, and, clutching Silver's lead tightly in his sweating paw, bow to the assembled masses. Silver's tail remained firmly slung between his back legs.

Both Sarah and Anthony had entered (however unwillingly) into the atmosphere of the whole thing. They smiled hollowly at one another and then down at the dog. Silver looked miserable. Sarah frowned and then whispered to Anthony, 'What's wrong with him? Normally he loves applause and attention, he adores a crowd.'

Anthony shook his head and shrugged. He tweaked at Silver's lead, but Silver didn't respond. Instead he seemed to be deeply preoccupied, squinting, wrinkling up his nose, shaking his head, acting as though he was in some kind of terrible discomfort.

Sarah and Anthony stared at each other worriedly. Silver inhaled deeply, and then, like a temperamental powder keg, let out a sneeze of an almost terrifying violence and ferocity. The sneeze shot out of Silver's nostrils, bounced around the four corners of the hall like an airy bullet, and then seemed to return to the stage and gave the appearance of thwacking Silver in the centre of his nose. Silver staggered, coughed, sniffed and snorted, then his nose began, unmistakably, to bleed. The blood didn't drip, it gushed.

Anthony dropped Silver's lead and fell to his knees beside the dog, his eyes damp with guilty tears. He said, 'Oh Sarah, what's wrong with him? What have I done? This is all my fault, if I hadn't been so selfish of late . . .'

Sarah shook her head, and, grabbing hold of his right arm, pulled Anthony up on to his feet again and into a tight embrace. She said, 'We've both been selfish, Anthony. We've both been rather childish recently, rather preoccupied. Maybe we haven't been properly receptive to Silver's needs during all this fuss and bother. But at least now we know where our priorities lie. This must make a difference, must wake us up to our obligations and responsibilities, both to him and to each other.'

Anthony felt his head clear. He said, 'I feel as though I've been lying in a big pot full of concrete these past few months, frozen, burdened, alone, but now the weight has been lifted. Sarah, I love you, I've always loved you. I want to try again, to make a new start with you and Silver.'

Sarah hugged him, confining the heavy weight of his midriff in her soft, alabaster arms. She said, 'God knows I've missed you, Anthony. This is a new beginning.'

A pool of blood surrounded Silver, but the crowd continued to clap and cheer. They couldn't see the blood flowing on to the red carpet, only the pale fur of the dogs and the embracing couple.

The other dogs sniffed at the pool of blood with speculative interest. One of them tasted it with the tip of his tongue and then withdrew.

Dual Balls

Selina Mitchell had never been particularly free-thinking. Since she was fifteen she had been completely under the sway of her dominant and rather single-minded husband Tom and her dominant and rather light-headed friend Joanna. She had always lived in Grunty Fen. If you grow up somewhere with a name like Grunty Fen you never really see the humour in the name, and Selina was no exception to this rule. She never thought it was a particularly amusing place to live. In fact she hated it most of the time. It was physically small, socially small and intellectually small. It wasn't even close enough to Cambridge to bask in any of the reflected glory; but if ever Selina had cause to write a letter to London or Manchester or Edinburgh for any reason she invariably wrote her address as *Grunty Fen, Cambridgeshire*. She hoped that this created a good impression.

The only scandal that had ever caused real consternation, discussion and debate in Grunty Fen was when Harry Fletcher had started to wear Wellington boots to school (in summer) and the school had been forced to alter their uniform rules in order to acknowledge that Wellingtons were a legitimate item of clothing for school wear. The teachers had seen this new allowance as a victory for the environment over the purity of education, a muddying of the intellectual pursuit. The kids all wore wellies to school for a while and then switched back to mucky trainers after their initial *joie de vivre* had worn off.

Selina had been a quick-witted student – by Grunty Fen standards – and had been one of the few children at the village school bright and determined enough to go to teacher training college. At seventeen she had packed her suitcase and had gone to Reading to learn how to be a teacher; to spread discipline and information.

At seventeen she had thought that she would never return to

Grunty Fen again, but inevitably she went home during her vacations to visit her parents and wrote long, emotional letters to her boyfriend Tom, who had tried to stop her going to college in the first place by asking her to marry him.

After three years at college Selina had returned to Grunty Fen, 'Just until I decide where I really want to go.' Eventually she had married Tom and had started teaching at the village primary school.

She disliked children and didn't want any of her own. Tom liked children – probably because he wasn't forced into a classroom with thirty of them every day – but he realized that if he wanted to hang on to Selina (she was one of the intellectual élite) then he would have to bow to her better judgement.

Time rolled by. Selina's life was as flat as the fens and just about as interesting. Nothing much happened at all.

Joanna, Selina's best friend, had lived a very similar sort of life except that she had enjoyed little success at school and had never attended teacher training college. She had got married at sixteen to John Burger whose family owned a large farm to the north of Grunty Fen, and had borne him two children before she reached twenty. She had always been wild and mischievous, but in a quiet way, a way that pretended that nothing serious was ever going on, or at least nothing seriously bad. Joanna was the bale of hay in Selina's field. She made Selina's landscape moderately more entertaining.

Joanna didn't really know the meaning of hard work. Most country women throw in their lot with their husbands and work like automatons on the farm. But Joanna had more sense than that. She preferred to stay at home 'creating a friendly home environment' and cultivating her good looks.

At the age of thirty-nine she aspired to the Dallas lifestyle. She spent many hours growing and painting her nails, making silk-feel shirts and dresses on her automatic sewing machine and throwing or attending Tupperware parties.

Joanna was Grunty Fen's only hedonist, but hedonism wasn't just her way of life, it was her religion, and she tried to spread it like a spoonful of honey on buttery toast.

*

They were in a café in Ely, a stone's throw from the cathedral, eating a couple of cream eclairs with coffee. Selina was making fun of Joanna but Joanna didn't seem to mind. She pulled the chocolate away from the choux pastry with her cake fork as Selina said laughingly, 'I still can't think of that birthday without smiling. My fortieth, and I thought it would be some sort of great landmark. I was so depressed. I opened Tom's present and it was a home first aid kit. Of course I said how lovely it was. Then, trying to hide my disappointment, I opened your present, firmly believing that it would contain something frivolous and feminine. But inside the parcel there were only ten odd pieces of foam, all neatly and pointlessly sewed up around the edges. Neither of us knew what the hell they were. I thought they might be miniature cushions without covers. Tom thought they were for protecting your knees during cricket games, a sort of knee guard. I even thought they might be falsies.'

Joanna smiled. 'This must be one of the only places in the world where a woman of forty doesn't understand the basics of sophisticated dressing. I thought you could sew the shoulder pads into all your good shirts and dresses. It's a fashionable look, Selina, honestly.'

Selina shrugged her non-padded shoulders. 'I will sew them in eventually, I promise.'

Joanna grinned to herself. She looked rather cheery. Usually before, during and after the consumption of a cream cake Joanna panicked about its calory content and moaned about its probable effect on her midriff.

As Selina waited for the inevitable outburst she said, 'If we didn't come to Ely every few weeks for a chat and a break I'm sure I'd go mad. Ely. Imagine! This small, insignificant town has come to symbolize freedom and independence to me. It's rather sad; it's like the Americans symbolizing freedom with a sparrow instead of a bald eagle.'

She looked into Joanna's face. Joanna was smiling. It was as if she was listening to a song that no one else could hear. Selina stared at her in silence for a minute or so and then said, 'What is it, Joanna? I'm sure you're up to something.'

Joanna's eyes were vaguely glassy. Selina frowned. 'You've not been taking those tranquillizers again, have you?'

Joanna laughed. It was a sort of throaty, gutsy laugh. 'Oh Selina, if only you knew. If only! What's Tom like in bed at the moment? Has it improved since our last little chat?'

Selina shrugged and her cheeks reddened. 'Nothing much has happened in that department. Are you enjoying that cake?'

She had finished hers several minutes before, but Joanna was still (uncharacteristically) pushing her cake around her plate. Selina added quickly – to distract Joanna from intimate territory – 'School's been awful. Felicity has been sitting in on classes. It's to do with the new assessment rules from the education authority. The classroom is no longer my kingdom. It's been taken over by men in little grey suits. Of course Felicity loves it all. She even had the cheek to offer me a few tips on my teaching technique the other day. I'm surprised she was capable of taking any of the lesson in. Most of it she spent fiddling with her hearing aid. Anyway, everyone knows that Heads are incapable of controlling classes and that's why they become Heads in the first place. Maybe I'm just bitter, but the thought of that old crone deigning to tell me how to handle a class! She said something like, "Be freer, Selina, be more adventurous, take risks!" I tried to tell her that the syllabus had destroyed all elements of spontaneity in the classroom. If the kids want to cope with the workload nowadays it's all blackboard, chalk and copying.'

As Selina finished speaking Joanna shuddered slightly. Selina smiled. 'Ghost walk over your grave?'

Joanna shook her head and then giggled furtively. 'Look Selina, it's not that I'm not interested in what you are saying about school – God knows, my two did well enough under your tuition and they thought you were a great teacher – it isn't that I'm not interested, but I just must change the subject for a moment.'

As Joanna spoke, she leaned towards Selina conspiratorially and her voice dropped to a whisper, 'Selina, I'm wearing Dual Balls.'

Selina frowned. 'What do you mean? Is it a girdle of some kind, or some sort of skin ointment?'

Joanna never ceased to amaze her with her violent enthusiasms and frivolity. She pushed a slightly greying brown curl behind her ear and thought abstractedly, 'I must have my hair cut, it's almost touching my shoulders now.'

Joanna's chair scraped along the floor as she pulled it up closer to Selina. Selina could smell her perfume – something heady like Opium – which flushed through the air like bleach through water. Joanna whispered again, 'I've got Dual Balls, Selina. I've had them in since I left the house. It's been incredible.'

Selina shrugged, 'You're going to have to explain this to me, Joanna. I don't know what Dual Balls are.'

Joanna bit her lip and stared at Selina through her heavily mascaraed lashes for a moment, then she said, 'I got them from an underwear catalogue. I ordered them and they came in the post. John doesn't know anything about them.'

Selina cleared her throat nervously, 'Are they something rude, Joanna?' Joanna winked saucily. 'I should say so. They're like two small round vibrating grapes. Battery operated.'

Selina took a sip of her coffee to try and deflate the tension, then said, 'Have you got them in your bag?'

Joanna snorted loudly and several people at other tables turned and stared at them both for a moment. Selina felt slightly embarrassed. Joanna soon recovered from her fit of hilarity and whispered, 'They're not in my bag, stupid. I've got them in my fanny.'

Selina was not initially so much shocked by the idea of Joanna's little vibrating grapes as by her casual use of the word 'fanny'. It was an old-fashioned word. She had once had a great aunt called Fanny, a gregarious, light-hearted aunt who had always seemed very old to her as a child; old, frail but charming.

She didn't really know how to reply to Joanna, how to disguise her intense unease and embarrassment. Luckily Joanna had other things on her mind. After a few seconds silence she squeezed Selina's arm and said, 'I'm going to nip into the toilets and take them out, then you can have a proper look at them.'

Selina's expression was querulous. Joanna noticed as she stood up, and grinned. 'Don't worry, Selina, I'll give them a good wash before you have to have any contact with them.'

Selina sighed. 'Joanna, please be discreet. This is only Ely after all, not San Francisco.'

Joanna didn't reply.

Once she'd gone Selina relaxed and drank a large mouthful of her coffee. She stared out of the window at the cathedral. She thought, 'God, I feel old. Maybe it's teaching. It just beats all the enthusiasm out of you. I'm sure I never used to feel this way. The kids are no better or no worse than they were twenty years ago. It must be me that's changed.' She sighed and waited for Joanna's return.

After about five minutes Joanna emerged from the toilets looking furtive but self-satisfied, like a large tom cat on the prowl, about to spray an unsuspecting territory with his rank odour. Selina thought, 'This room belongs to Joanna. She doesn't give a damn about anything.'

Joanna sat down next to her again and Selina said straight away, 'I don't know where you get these ideas from – or your nerve for that matter – look at you, as bold as brass!'

Joanna smiled and patted her chestnut perm with one of her bright-pink-fingernailed hands, 'Don't look at this hand, look at the other one under the table.'

Selina moved backwards slightly and stared down at Joanna's other hand which held the Dual Balls like a couple of freshly laid eggs. Selina said, 'They're bigger than I thought they'd be and attached to each other. I imagined that they'd be a sort of flesh colour, not that strange off-white.'

Joanna raised her eyebrows, 'Flesh *is* off-white, Selina. Are Tom's balls a very different colour to these?'

She smiled provocatively. Selina shook her head disapprovingly. 'Tom's . . .' – she couldn't use the word – 'Tom's aren't anything unusual, Joanna, and I certainly don't make a habit of trying to use them like you've just used those. Also, his don't use batteries and they aren't attached by a small piece of cord.'

Joanna smirked. 'You wish Tom's balls were like these. They're very effective, and so discreet. I think the thrill of using them is trebled by the fact of wearing them out. It's so arousing.'

Selina grimaced. 'Walking can't be easy with them in. Why don't they just drop out?'

As Selina spoke Joanna switched the balls on. She waited for Selina to finish talking and then said, 'Why don't you try them and see?' The balls vibrated vigorously in her hand. They sounded like a quieter version of an electric razor. Selina was sure that everyone could hear. She whispered frantically, 'For God's sake Joanna, switch them off.' Joanna frowned. 'I worry about you, Selina. You're becoming very old-maidish, very schoolmarmish. You don't have any spirit of adventure any more.'

Selina didn't rise to the bait. 'I've never had any spirit of adventure and you know it.'

Joanna nodded. 'I suppose that's true. No backbone, no spontaneity. No interest in what's state of the art . . .'

Selina raised an eyebrow. 'Where did you come across that little phrase? Something on television, something American I suppose?'

'You wouldn't have the nerve to wear these out, no way,' Joanna interrupted.

Selina smiled. 'I'd have enough nerve, Joanna, just too much sense. I don't need something like those. I think they're horrible. Now switch them off.'

Joanna turned and stared out of the window at people passing by. An old lady staggered past pulling her shopping trolley. Joanna pointed at the woman, 'I bet she'd wear them out. I bet she's got more spunk in her little finger than you've got in your entire body.'

Selina almost smiled at this but then stopped herself. 'Possibly. Look, the waitress is coming over with the bill. Please turn them off.'

Joanna didn't turn them off, but started instead to lift up the hand containing the vibrating balls until they were almost at a level with the surface of the table. Selina was excruciatingly embarrassed. 'Joanna, switch them off and put them away. You're embarrassing me.'

Joanna was staring at the Dual Balls rather thoughtfully. After a moment she said, 'I dare you to wear these when you're teaching one of your classes. Just for one lesson. I dare you!'

Joanna loved dares. This was principally because she always thought of them and didn't therefore usually do them herself. 'Go on Selina, I dare you!'

Selina laughed. 'You've got to be kidding. Those horrible little things are having no contact with my intimate body whatsoever.'

Joanna lifted the balls slightly higher than the table and said, 'If you don't accept the dare I swear I'm going to put these into your coffee cup when the waitress comes to clear the table. That should be in about twenty seconds.'

Selina saw a couple of people at the nearest table to them discussing something and laughing. She was sure that they had noticed. She said, 'Joanna, put them down, please.'

Joanna held them even higher. The waitress started to walk towards them. When she was about five steps from the table Selina said, 'OK, I promise to wear them, I promise, all right?'

Joanna switched the balls off immediately. It seemed very quiet without their buzzing.

On her way home Joanna passed John in the tractor. He stopped so that she could overtake him then waved his arm so that she would pause for a moment. She wound down her window. 'Yes?'

He shouted from his high seat, not bothering to switch off the tractor's roaring engine, 'Did she take them?'

Joanna nodded emphatically. 'Yes. It worked like a dream. She was really shocked when she thought that I was wearing them. It was a real effort not to laugh.'

He smiled. 'You must be a great actress then.'

She shrugged. 'I did all right.'

She crossed her fingers down by the steering wheel. He frowned – although he couldn't see her hands – 'Joanna, you were just acting?' Joanna guffawed. 'Don't be ridiculous. I'd probably have crashed the car if I'd worn them driving . . . Of course I wouldn't dream of wearing them anyway, why should I?'

She winked. He smiled. He obviously believed her. She uncrossed her fingers, waved at him and then drove on.

She negotiated the turn into their driveway with special care; she'd almost driven off the road there on the trip out.

One of the favourite pastimes in Grunty Fen is Chinese Whispers. People whisper gossip like it's going out of season. They also discuss what's happened in all of the major soaps and mini-series on television. Mostly though they prefer to gossip because it's a tiny place and everyone knows everyone else's business.

John got pissed in the local pub on Saturday night and told several of his cronies about Joanna's dare. The men all laughed loudly at the notion of someone as staid and strait-laced as Selina experimenting with sexual gadgets. They knew she wouldn't do it, but they enjoyed thinking about it just the same. A couple of them went home in their cups and told their wives. The women were shocked, interested and surprised on the whole; a small proportion were slightly jealous.

After Sunday lunch Selina was doing the washing up in the kitchen and Tom was sitting at the dining table in the next room doing the *Sunday Telegraph* crossword. Occasionally he read out loud to Selina any of the clues that had completely eluded him.

Selina washed the soapsuds from the final plate and placed it with the others on the drying rack. Tom seemed busy and preoccupied so she took this opportunity to clean out the sink and refill it with very hot water and a squirt of bleach. She went and found her handbag and took out the Dual Balls which she had placed inside, wrapped up in a tissue. She opened the tissue and removed the Dual Balls then placed them in the hot water and bleach, still wearing her rubber gloves. As she rubbed the balls with her hands she felt like a fetishist.

At the sound of Tom's voice from the next room she jumped guiltily and her heart lurched; then in a split second she had grabbed the washing-up cloth and had dropped it over the balls, covering them completely. Tom was saying, 'Thirty-one across. Vulgar

Cockney squeezes ends of these into tube. Six letters. I think it's an anagram. Any ideas, Selina?'

At this exact moment, a mile or so away, Joanna and John were still eating their lunch of beef and roast potatoes. John had a slight hangover. Joanna had prepared a meal for four but neither of the children had bothered hanging around for it. This made John even more ill-tempered and grouchy. He kept saying, 'It's such a waste of good food. Those two don't know what it's like to do without. You spoil them.'

Joanna ignored him. She was thinking about Selina and the Dual Balls. She wondered whether she would use them or not. Selina rarely broke her word, if ever.

She cut into a potato and watched the steam rise from its hot centre. She speared a bit of it on to her fork and prepared to put it into her mouth. Before she had done so, however, John said, 'I told a couple of the fellas about your joke with Selina last night.'

Joanna stared at him, dumbstruck. 'You did what?'

Her voice was sharp and strident. He shrugged. 'I know I promised not to but it sort of slipped out.'

She put down her fork. 'I don't know why I tell you anything. You're totally unreliable. I'm sick of you spreading my business about and sticking your nose into everything. This was none of your affair in the first place.'

He frowned. 'Well, why did you tell me about it then?'

She pushed her chair back from the table and stood up. 'I didn't tell you about it, you opened my bloody mail. You have no right to open letters and parcels that are addressed to me.'

He shook his head, confused. 'You don't have anything to hide from me, Joanna. What's the problem all of a sudden? This isn't like you.'

Joanna slammed her hand down on the table, rattling the plates and glasses and cutlery. 'I am a woman, John, women have secrets. That's one of the few good things about being a woman as far as I can see. Now that you've told everyone about this thing with Selina she'll be a laughing stock. She's my friend, for God's sake.'

John stood up and moved around the table towards Joanna. His head ached with every twitch of his body. 'Everyone knows that Selina won't use those things. She's not like that. It was a silly idea in the first place really.'

Joanna felt tearful. She shouted, 'Well, it seemed like a good excuse at the time!'

Then, grabbing her plate, she marched off into the kitchen, where she threw her lunch into the bin.

John sat down at the table again. He felt somewhat confused.

Felicity Barrow received a telephone call from her friend Janet Street on Sunday afternoon. Janet was extremely excited because she had a bit of amusing gossip to impart about one of the teachers at Felicity's school. Felicity liked to call it 'my school', even though she was only the headmistress.

Janet had a rather puffy, breathy, light voice, and the scandal in her news almost extinguished it altogether. She gasped down the phone, 'Jim told me that Selina Mitchell has been wearing some sort of sexual device to school and using it while she's teaching classes.' Felicity interrupted, putting on her best head-teacherish voice. 'What on earth are you saying, Janet? And do speak clearly, I haven't adjusted my hearing aid yet.' On concluding this sentence she sipped her tea and took a large bite out of a mint-flavoured Viscount biscuit.

Janet gulped. This noise travelled all the way down the telephone line and into Felicity's ear. Then she whispered, 'Well, Jim said that it is a sort of vibrating machine which is shaped like the female sexual organs, but convex. It is attached by elastic to the two thighs, I think the elastic goes around the buttocks at the back . . . anyway Jim says it's very discreet. What happens is that it is battery-operated and it presses into the vagina while methodically rubbing at the clitoris. Apparently after several minutes this stimulates a sexual climax.'

Felicity tried to suppress the impulse to laugh, but finally gave into a throaty chuckle. 'Janet, I think what you're saying is untrue. We both know Selina Mitchell, we've both known her for years. I was headmistress at Grunty Fen Primary when she was a pupil at the school herself. There has never been anyone in the school whose dignity, discretion and professionalism I have held in higher regard. Just the other day I sat in on her class and assessed her performance. My only advice to her was that I thought her techniques too staid, perhaps a jot unimaginative . . .'

Janet interrupted. 'That's all well and good, Felicity, but you know what they say, there's no smoke without fire. She did go away at the end of the sixties, after all. Who knows what sort of habits she picked up then . . .'

Felicity's initial amused indulgence at Janet's news suddenly evaporated. She snapped, 'Stop talking such absolute rubbish, Janet. I'd certainly have expected that you of all people would be the last to surrender your credulity to the clutches of vicious and totally unfounded gossip. I don't want to hear anything more about this subject, and if I do hear anything from a different source I will be forced to presume that it originated with you. Do I make myself clear?' Janet answered breathlessly in the affirmative and the conversation ended abruptly shortly afterwards.

Felicity had been headmistress at Grunty Fen Primary for almost thirty years. The time had come and gone for her to retire but she had ignored suggestions from various departments – chiefly from her husband Donald, who was several years into retirement himself – and had carried on giving her all to the young children of the district.

She took her vocation very seriously. Her main problem was that she couldn't be convinced that anyone else she knew would be suitable for her job. The ideal candidate would be a woman – she thought that women made the best Heads because they were much more frightening than men – and preferably they would originate from Grunty Fen or the surrounding area. She believed that Fen children had to be taught by people who were familiar with the various interests, problems and subtleties of their character. She knew that Selina Mitchell was keen for promotion. She had been coolly vetted for a favourable reference from Selina herself on several occasions, but nothing had come of it.

Felicity put her feet up on to her foot-stool, took out her hearing aid, leaned back in her chair and took another bite out of her biscuit. She had resented Janet's news because she felt that anything bad said about her staff reflected badly on the school and ultimately on herself. She was rather proud and vain but disliked these qualities in other people. Selina, she believed, was far too proud and vain for her own good. She was too closed, not sufficiently free-thinking. Felicity found her distant and arrogant. Selina found Felicity interfering and arrogant. Neither side would bow down to the other. They weren't destined to be good friends, but Felicity often regretted that they had never even managed to become formal friends.

She took another sip of tea and decided to call Selina into her office for a serious chat first thing in the morning. She picked up a copy of the *People's Friend* and ran her finger down the list of contents, muttering. 'No smoke without fire, indeed!'

Selina didn't dare carry the Dual Balls to school in her teaching bag in case any of the children poked around in it looking for a pencil or a book and came across them. Instead she wore a smart blue blazer with a deep inside pocket in which she carefully placed the Dual Balls before breakfast.

On arriving at school she went straight into her classroom to enjoy five minutes of quiet contemplation before the start of the day. She was keen to avoid Felicity and other members of staff, who on a Monday morning always seemed to try extra hard to be sociable and community spirited. Selina hated all that 'bonding' business. It wasn't her style. She rarely went out for drinks on a Friday night with her colleagues; even so, she always saw them over the weekend because Grunty Fen and the surrounding areas were so sparsely populated that a trip to the shops usually meant a trip to meet everyone from your past, your present and your future that you were keen to avoid.

She sat at her desk and put her hand into her inside pocket to feel the Dual Balls. They felt cold and smooth; highly unerotic. She looked around the classroom and thought, 'I'm so bloody sick of this routine. I'm sick of teaching. I just wish that it was heading somewhere or that something would come of it, but nothing will. I've vegetated, stultified.'

The room smelled clean but of chalk and paper and dust. Her mind turned to Joanna and their conversation at the weekend. This raised a smile. She thought, 'Of course she's right. I don't have any real spirit of adventure.'

The bell rang and the day began.

Felicity had popped into the staff room at the beginning of the day to ask Selina into her office for a chat. Unfortunately Selina didn't materialize so Felicity had to content herself with the idea of meeting her during lunchtime. She checked the wall chart in the staff room to make sure that Selina wasn't on play or dinner duty.

It was a hot day. After several hours Selina became uncomfortable in her blazer and took it off so that she could cool down, hanging it carefully over the top of her chair and keeping a firm eye on it. The morning droned on and eventually it was time for lunch.

All morning she'd had half of her mind on the Dual Balls. A part of her really wanted to fulfil her dare and show Joanna that she was a woman of her word. Another part of her baulked at the idea of using the balls in principle. They were crude and revolting. Secretly she was rather interested to know how they would feel, but only in a silly, inquisitive way that took no account of what was right or for the best.

As the last child left her classroom Selina made a firm decision. She resolved to go and 'try on' the Dual Balls and to try them out for several minutes in the privacy of her classroom at the beginning of her lunch hour. Then, if Joanna asked, she could say in all honesty that she had in fact worn the balls at school in the classroom.

The day was very still and warm. She opened the top button on her shirt to let the air circulate more freely around her throat then strolled to her chair and put on her blue blazer. It felt heavy and made her skin feel sticky. She felt ridiculously tense and strung-out. Luckily the toilets were close to her classroom. She worried about walking with the Dual Balls in; Joanna hadn't cleared up that little chestnut during their coffee and eclairs.

The toilets were empty. She chose one of the two cubicles and locked herself in. She was glad that she had opted to wear a skirt and sheer stockings for easier access.

Inserting the Dual Balls gave her a feeling of youthful mischievousness, as though she were one of the children in school doing something secretive and wrong like puffing on a cigarette.

The Dual Balls felt cold, bulky and stupid. She pulled the string that switched them on. In her hyper-sensitive state the buzzing of the Balls seemed like the violent crashing of cymbals. Although the toilets were empty apart from herself, she coughed loudly with embarrassment to try and hide the initial shock of the sound.

After a few moments of acclimatization Selina rearranged her clothing and stepped out of the cubicle. The balls felt like an inordinately large blue-bottle whizzing around, lost inside her knickers. She took a few experimental steps around by the sinks – where she fastidiously washed her hands – and the Dual Balls stayed firmly in place. She breathed a sigh of relief, then steeled her resolve and nerve as she headed for the door.

Once out in the corridor, surrounded by screaming, sweaty, excitable, break-enjoying children, Selina was able to relax. She felt less furtive and guilty out in the public sphere. She reached her classroom without misadventure; though her variation on a John Wayne swagger may easily have aroused interest in any but a child's mind. She pushed open her classroom door and went in.

Her heart sank. Sitting in the front row of desks, dead centre, was Felicity Barrow.

Smiling broadly, Felicity said, 'Oh good, Selina. I was just about to give up my search and return to the staff room.'

Selina's entire body felt stiff and immobile; only the Dual Balls continued on moving naturally inside her. She tried to negotiate the walk to her desk as freely and casually as possible. To distract Felicity's attention she said, 'Lovely day isn't it?', and pointed towards the window. Felicity turned towards the window and stared out through it at the blue sky. 'Yes, it is lovely.'

She was pleased that Selina was trying to be friendly. Selina took these few seconds' leeway to trot over to her desk and plop herself down on to her hard wooden chair. She noisily cleared her throat so that Felicity's silent contemplation of the day's glory wouldn't emphasize the jubilant buzzing of the Dual Balls. Felicity's gaze returned to Selina's face. 'You're looking very well, Selina, if I may say so, very bright.' Selina smiled. 'I think I'm actually just a bit warm. Perhaps I should take my blazer off.'

She performed this simple action with as much 'involved noise' as possible, concluding with the scraping up of her chair closer to the table. Her hands were shaking slightly, so she took hold of a pencil and tapped out a tiny, slight rhythm with it on the table top.

Felicity watched these adjustments very closely, then said, 'You seem unusually tense today, Selina, any particular reason?'

Selina shrugged. Inside she was boiling with embarrassment and unease but she endeavoured not to let this show. 'I don't know, Felicity. I feel all right really, just a bit, I don't know, a bit frustrated, rudderless . . .'

She didn't really know what she was saying, but after she had said it she felt as though she was talking about sex, as though she was an actress in a dirty blue film. She pinched herself and blinked her eyes, then looked over at Felicity.

Felicity was still smiling at her. 'Maybe you're upset about all that ridiculous gossip that was circulating this weekend?'

Selina was still recovering from the tingling pain of her self-inflicted pinch. The pain seemed rather arousing, and the discomfort too. She asked automatically, 'What gossip?'

Felicity's cheeks reddened slightly. She had hoped that Selina would have been willing to make this conversation easy and unembarrassing. She cleared her throat and to hide her discomfort adjusted the position of her hearing aid in her ear. 'Apparently someone has been spreading a rumour about . . . about your purported use of sexual stimulants during school time.'

Selina's face flushed violently and her jaw went slack, 'I . . . I don't know what to say Felicity. What can I say?'

At that moment in time she felt as though her head was clouding over, clouding up, as though she were in a plane that was going through turbulent clouds. She felt quite willing to admit to every-thing.

Whatever doubts had clouded Felicity's mind evaporated immedi-ately when she saw the strength of Selina's reaction. She had expected Selina to keep her cool and to utter a cold, cynical, stinging reply. Instead her reply was so unguarded and natural, so loose and out of character, almost intimate, that Felicity could not stop herself from smiling warmly at her. 'Of course I knew it was untrue. I just thought you should be aware of the kind of things that a couple of nasty people are saying.'

Selina couldn't meet Felicity's gaze. She looked down at her desk and tried to call on an inner reserve of strength. Unfortunately this moment of introspection only re-emphasized in her mind the furtive activities of the Dual Balls. She was so tense that her body had become extremely dynamic and excitable. The hard wooden chair wasn't helping matters either. She shuddered, and suddenly her brain felt like sherbet.

The strength of Selina's reaction made Felicity's heart twist in sympathy. She bit her lip for a moment and said nervously, 'Selina, I'm sorry. I didn't think that this would affect you so badly.'

Selina felt as though she was on a roller-coaster ride. She said, 'I feel as though I'm on a roller-coaster ride, Felicity. I don't know what to say.'

She was all gaspy and uncontrolled, her insides churning with a sort of ecstatic violence. In the silence of the room she heard herself breathing heavily. Felicity sat quietly, saying nothing.

After a minute or so Selina began to gasp. She was totally out of control. She threw her head down on the table and shuddered until the shudders turned into enormous, violent, gasping, wracking howls.

Felicity froze. She had never seen such a forthright display of uninhibited emotion before and from, of all people, Selina Mitchell. She felt a terrible sense of guilt that she should have provoked such a display, but also a sense of pride that Selina should have chosen to share this wild moment of release and abandon with her, Felicity. She stood up and went over to Selina's side and placed a gentle hand on her back which she moved up and down, up and down, as though comforting a small child or burping a baby.

Selina felt Felicity's hand massaging her back but felt too far gone to respond coherently. She just said, 'Oh God, oh no, oh my!'

Felicity moved her hand from Selina's back and grasped hold of one of her hands. She said, 'Selina, listen to me. This isn't as bad as it seems to you. It doesn't affect the respect and regard that I have for your teaching abilities. You are one of my best members of staff, in fact you are my very best member of staff.'

Selina heard Felicity's words but their sounds washed over her and made very little sense. She was at the edge of a precipice and in the next moment she was falling, flailing, floating. Her ears tingled as the wind rushed by. She steeled herself for a crash landing, but instead her landing was cushioned by a million feather eiderdowns, each as soft as a poodle's belly. Everything solidified again.

Felicity was pleased to note that after a minute or so her piece of encouragement had appeared to get through to Selina. She was calming down. After a while her breathing returned to normal and she raised her head slightly from the desk. Several seconds later she said quietly, 'Felicity, I feel terrible about this, but it was just out of my control. I feel so embarrassed.'

Felicity clucked her tongue and shook her head, 'Don't be silly, Selina. I know how these things build up. I'm just glad that you were able to let go of all that anguish and to share it with me.'

Selina felt as though she was floating in the Red Sea, lifted above the water by the sodium chloride, the sea like a big marshmallow. She blinked several times and sat up straight. She noticed that Felicity was still holding her hand. She smiled at Felicity and said, 'Things have been building up inside me for a long time. I feel so much better now, so buoyant.'

Felicity gave Selina's hand one final squeeze and then let go. She said, 'I know that you are a very controlled person, Selina. I've known you for most of your life and you've never let your emotions rule your head. I think you very much deserved this opportunity to vent your feelings.'

Selina was now fully recovered. She felt stupid but also surprisingly smug. She said, 'I hope you don't think that this silly outburst will have any bearing on my discipline and dignity before my classes.' Felicity shook her head. 'I know that I can always rely on you, Selina. I'm certainly quite positive that you are an indispensable asset to this school.'

Inside Felicity's head an idea was turning. It was as though a light had been switched on or the last piece of a jigsaw puzzle snapped into place. She said, 'Trust me, Selina, you have a great future ahead of you at this school. I'm going to see to that.'

Selina began to smile. She said, 'Felicity, you've been very kind and very understanding. Thank you.'

Felicity shrugged, 'It was nothing. Now clear up your face. Here's a tissue. A bit of spit and polish should do the job.'

Selina took the proffered tissue and applied it to her running mascara. Felicity walked towards the door. 'This has been an invaluable chat, Selina.'

Selina nodded and pushed her hair behind her ears, 'It has, Felicity, and thanks again.'

Felicity smiled and opened the door. Before she closed it behind her, however, she turned and said somewhat distractedly, 'I'm sorry to rush off like this, Selina, but my hearing aid is playing me up. I think it's dust or the batteries. It's been driving me mad with its buzzing for the last fifteen minutes or so.'

Selina smiled. 'That's all right.'

As the door closed, she stuffed Felicity's tissue into her mouth and bit down hard.

John's Box

A story for Manuel

This story is about two people who talk to each other. One of them is dying. The dying man is called John. The girl is Melissa. Melissa works in a clothes shop. They become friends.

John cradled his head in his hands and said, almost to himself, 'I can't believe I'm dying. I'm only thirty-four. I feel so fucking helpless.'

The doctor stood behind him and placed a comforting hand on his shoulder. The hand felt like a vice, like the vice of death, closing in on him, tightening. He left the hospital and went shopping.

Shopping was his excuse. It was his way of expressing how he felt. Throughout his thirty-four years he had knowingly frittered away his wages – earned through selling advertising space in newspapers – at shops in the centre of London. Oxford Street was his Mecca, Regent Street his Lourdes. He simply adored Liberty's but felt ashamed of this adoration. It seemed dangerously effeminate to enjoy looking at bottles of preserves, bits of jewellery, pyjamas and ties, crockery and glass, so, so much.

At home he had five tea sets and three complete dinner services, although he rarely entertained. He was too busy shopping to make friends, too busy feeling ashamed about expressing himself solely through this act of exchange.

He was bright. At school he had been encouraged in both the arts and the sciences. Yet his favourite lesson had always been woodwork. When he was fourteen he had built a bookshelf entirely under his own steam and had received top marks for his initiative and effort. When he was fourteen. Now he was thirty-four and sold advertising space for a living and was dying and had a small rented house in Mile End and had no one to love him.

He owned lots of things. He had many suits, records, books, bits of sculpture and ornamentation dotted liberally around on the tables and shelves in his front room at home. A beautiful three-piece suite. He even had a dishwasher.

As he walked along Charing Cross Road, thinking about buying some books as a distraction, placing his hand in his pocket to feel the money, various coins and notes pressed next to his thigh, the thought popped into his head that he had done nothing with his life. The things he had bought would stay in the house when he died. They would either be sold or left. Who would want them? All the things he had bought, all those hours spent searching and queuing and working and earning and buying. All for nothing.

He veered a sharp left into Boots and picked up some shaving cream – made with coconut and honey – and stood by the counter with a five-pound-note in his hand. The girl behind the till had a badge on her lapel which read,

I am Sandra.
May I help you?

She took the shaving cream, put it into a bag and said, 'That's three pounds twenty please.'

She looked into the man's eyes. He was young, early thirties, with brown hair and a thin face. High cheekbones. His hand was shaking. She put out her hand to receive his money and he said, 'I can't believe I'm doing this. I have so many kinds of shaving cream at home. I've just been told that I'm dying, and my immediate reaction is to go out and buy shaving cream.'

He put his hand to his chin which was well shaven. Sandra watched him as his eyes filled with tears. She pulled her hand back and said, 'Don't buy this then. Go home and rest. You're probably still in a state of shock.'

The man wiped his eyes and smiled shakily. He offered her the money and said, 'I can't change the habits of a lifetime.'

She gave him his change and he thanked her.

When John got home he thought about telephoning his mother, who lived in Blackpool, to tell her his news. But each time he reached for the telephone his mouth went dry and he began to shake and sweat. It wasn't so much the idea of actually physically telling her that was so upsetting as the idea of how the news might affect her. He didn't want to interrupt whatever she was doing with the sharp ring of the phone and then to stutter some words at her about him, her son, dying. He couldn't do it. After some thought he resolved to write her a letter instead. There was something very complete and formal in the act of writing and receiving a letter. He also decided to write to his ex-girlfriend who had emigrated to Australia three years before. They were the only two people that he could think of to inform. The letters took an age to compose, but eventually it was done and he sat in front of the television and fell asleep with the remote control still in his hand.

There is a shop in west Soho patronized by the fashion-conscious, a glossy, gaudy bauble of a shop full of bright one-off designs, flamboyant jewellery and T-shirts with slogans on them that cost half a week's wages each. Melissa worked in this shop, and she loved it. Two of them worked there; Melissa and Steve. Steve was gay, funny, sharp and always wore imported Nike tracksuits. Melissa wore whatever she could afford with red lipstick and her short hair greased back, slicked back like a seal.

Melissa had studied fashion at college for a couple of years and Steve had been at art school. They were great friends. As with all high-fashion establishments, a certain amount of ironic exchange between the staff members concerning various customers was the order of the day. Melissa and Steve were about as bitchy and intimidating a team as it was possible to be. Much of their day was consumed by tasks like tea and coffee making, selecting and changing music tapes and trying on any of the new clothes that came into the shop before hanging them up in the designated way.

Steve would often be seen lolling on the till reading *The Age of Reason*, *Nausea*, or anything else by Sartre that took his fancy. Melissa read *Vogue* and *Elle*.

When they were especially bored they played games. One of the games was called 'Power Sell'. Steve had invented this game. The rules were that you had to sell a previously selected item – usually whatever was either the most expensive or the most gaudy and outrageous item in the shop – to the very next person that walked in after a selected time. No matter how small, large, fat, thin, tall, the person was, it had to be a particular item in a particular size. If after Power Selling an item they managed to secure a deal, then the other person bought lunch that day.

Another game they played that Melissa had invented was called 'Guess or Gush'. This game involved one of them agreeing to attempt to guess the profession of the next customer that came into the shop. After speaking to the person for a few seconds – 'May I help you? We have these in yellow and brown' – they would then walk to the till and write their ideas down on a scrap of paper. Next, the person who wasn't guessing would read the slip and approach the customer saying something like, 'Excuse me for being nosy, but don't you work (for example) in a hardware shop?' If the answer was affirmative then the person who had made the correct choice didn't have to make any tea or coffee for the next few days. If they were wrong, however, a penalty had to be paid, a kind of forfeit, and they were obliged to be degradingly obsequious to the customer, to gush and flatter. This forfeit was perceived as being highly humiliating by both of them. Steve always became extremely camp and hilarious under this sort of obligatory social pressure. Melissa would blush and rub the end of her nose self-consciously; a habit she had developed in her early teens.

In many ways this vulnerability made her much more endearing than she otherwise might be. She idealized some of the other hard-faced women that she knew who worked (in whatever capacity) in the fashion industry. At heart however she was just a big softy. Steve would often say this to her and would make it sound just about as complimentary as if she'd had bad breath. He'd put on a false Northern accent and say, 'Oooh! Our Lisa, you're a right big softy, you are,' and chuck her on the chin ever so gently.

At the heart of Melissa's character was a fundamental conflict, a paradox. Although she loved her life and what she had hitherto made of it – going to clubs with friends, knowing people who wrote for *The Face*, dropping names, spending money on clothes and, as Steve put it, 'Having a laff' – she felt as though at the centre of her life something very important was missing. There was a void, a space where her heart worked, a feeling of emptiness that she felt incapable of changing. She could be happy but never replete. The happiness came and went. It always depended on so much, and so much was random. She regularly wondered whether unhappiness – perhaps that is too strong a word for it – indifference, was simply a part of the human condition, the human make-up.

When she was fourteen she had tried to become a Catholic, wearing a crucifix and going to Mass. Eventually though, her fervour had faded and she'd laughed at herself and had felt foolish for wanting to belong. It was as though God, in his Catholic incarnation, had momentarily been an excuse, an alternative to sincerity or self awareness. God had not been Love, he had been a make-believe figure synonymous with passion and yet not passion. A cypher.

Whenever she concentrated too hard or too long on these dissatisfied thoughts – her inner sense of frustration and bewilderment – and became overwhelmingly maudlin as a consequence, Steve would take her out for a special lunch and have what he called 'One of Our Serious Chats'.

Although he was fond of Melissa he firmly believed that she was misguidedly intense. To him she seemed like a person caught in some sort of moral breakdown; as if there had been a kind of mental short circuit between her desires and her will. It was a complex idea but he endeavoured to explain it to her. He'd say, 'Think of it this way, Melissa. It's as though you are guided by a very strict and orthodox moral scheme, well, not so much guided because you don't act on it. I mean, it's as if your personality has been formed in a very precise way – you have a clear, lucid idea of right and wrong – yet nothing in your behaviour exhibits this belief. You are sincere, but your life isn't.'

Invariably Melissa would pick at her side salad and look confused. Eventually Steve would talk himself into circles and by the end of the meal he'd be saying, 'God, my life's such a mess. I'm so frivolous, just a bundle of pretentions and intentions. Ignore everything I've said. Have fun!'

At the mention of fun Melissa's heart would sink and she'd wonder if she could ever be happy. Steve would pay the bill and wonder whether he'd end up joining the Moonies.

The morning after his appointment at the hospital was a Tuesday. John resolved to phone in sick and take the day off work to sort himself out. He panicked at the idea of leaving work altogether though, because the days and weeks ahead of him were like an empty beach and his tide was coming in ever so surely but ever so slowly.

After telephoning he put on a jacket and picked up his letters. He wanted to post them straight away. He'd decided over breakfast that it must be easier to die if a selected number of people knew about it in advance. He hated the idea of keeping the knowledge of his illness inside him like an internal bruise, invisible but painful. He wanted a talking cure, or at least a talking cessation.

Because the weather was relatively fine he decided to walk a longer route to the post office. On his way he passed a school and two churches. As he passed by them he thought, 'I'll never be able to have children of my own. I'll not know God before I die. I won't come to terms with my life. I won't grow older and wiser and resigned.'

By the time he'd reached the Post Office he had listed fifty-seven things that he would never be able to do. He stood in the queue and touched the partition rope with the tips of his fingers, deep in thought. In front of him were several old women and a couple of old men. It was pension day. He thought, 'I'll never collect my pension.'

He tried to cheer himself up by thinking, 'Maybe everyone has lists of things they'll never do with their lives. In my case I just have a shorter time to compile my list. Some people have long, empty lives and all they ever do is to think about what it is that they haven't done.'

Even so, his eyes felt wet. The line was gradually getting shorter. In front of him most people were watching the large television advertising screen at the front of the queue which spouted out adverts for life insurance and special stamp collecting deals. John watched the screen and tried not to think.

After a few minutes the screen went blank and the words DEATH WITH DIGNITY appeared in bold, square, white letters. The image of a sad old woman emerged out of the blackness; she stared out at the queue with a desperate expression. She had dying eyes. John thought, 'I wonder if my eyes look like that now.'

A disembodied voice came out of the television. It said, 'Do you want to be a burden on your friends, family and loved ones when you die? No? Well then, why not prepare in advance?' Again DEATH WITH DIGNITY emerged over the image of the old woman. The letters sucked all colour from the screen and shrouded themselves in a funereal black backdrop.

John said the words to himself and they sounded so corny when he said them, like some silly, rhyming cliché coined to encapsulate the situation he now faced. They made him feel cheap and stupid.

The words faded again and the old woman's face reappeared. As her face came into focus this time, however, it broke into a smile. The camera moved to concentrate on her hand. In it she held a document. At the top of the document were the words DEATH WITH DIGNITY. Again the disembodied voice said, 'Why not prepare in advance? Pay for your funeral now, make your own choices, and we will deal with it in the future. Pick up a leaflet at the counter.'

A shutter came down inside John's head. He felt a sense of enormous negative power, an annihilating vigour. The next thing he knew he was out in the sunshine again and the letters were in his pocket, unstamped, unposted.

He stood still awhile, his head tilted towards the watery sun which shone on to his face and felt almost as though it had ironed out all the creases in his expression, all the lines and tiny crinkles. His first comprehensible thoughts were, 'It's not going to be like that for me. I'm not going to invest in my death as though it were simply another item, another purchase to be mulled over and paid for. It has to mean more than that.'

In the back of his mind he knew that his reaction was incoherent, almost hypocritical. A tiny mental shiver, an impulse, pumped in the rear of his brain which said, 'You've lived your thirty-four years this way, why not die this way too? Buy something, feel happy. Look at the options, make a decision, complete the deal. It's that simple.'

He turned his face from the sunlight and looked down at his hands which were clean and smooth with oval nails, pinky-brown and still strong. As he moved his fingers they tingled and he wondered how long he would be able to move them completely. He didn't know. He placed his hand in his pocket and felt the letters inside, then he felt for his wallet and got it out. Slowly an idea gelled together in his mind which made his stomach convulse and quiver with unease and excitement. He thought, 'That's it! I'm going to do it myself this time, I'm going to cut out the middleman just this once and create something that is truly individual.'

He opened his wallet, and as he did so he wondered where he could buy some wood locally. He felt like a kid again.

Steve had bought a copy of the American magazine *Vanity Fair* on his way to work that morning and had been reading it with great intensity for several hours. It was Tuesday. Melissa slunk around the shop, rearranging clothes, straightening clothes hangers, occasionally standing in the doorway and staring down the street in the intermittent sunlight. She felt distracted and miserable, not depressed though, it wasn't a physical thing beyond her control, it was more a conscious state of mind, a decision. She felt distracted and despondent, but didn't want to disturb Steve's reading with her melancholy.

Steve was reading an article about how Richard Gere was a Buddhist. Occasionally he would pass a comment about what he was reading. As she stood in the doorway he said, 'I'd never have thought Gere would be a Buddhist. He doesn't seem very serene or sincere. Apparently he spent quite a bit of time in a sort of monastery place in Tibet or somewhere.' Melissa sighed and said, 'Lots of stars are Buddhists. It involves chanting and candles and shit, doesn't it? I think Tina Turner was one. Maybe it was someone else, though.'

Steve looked up again. 'I think it was Tina. It changed her life after Ike.'

Melissa shrugged disinterestedly. Steve flicked through the pages again and then said, 'I read a really interesting thing in here this morning on the tube, about an American psychiatrist called Dr Death who travels around the country getting first-time killers the death penalty by saying that he knows and can guarantee that someone is going to kill again.'

Melissa carried on staring down the road. She said, 'That's weird. Surely it's impossible to tell whether someone is going to kill again, unless, I suppose, the person is mentally unbalanced.'

Steve stood up and rearranged the changing-room curtain. He said, 'No, it doesn't work like that. The whole point of him is that he testifies against first-time offenders, people who are apparently sane and have only murdered once. He uses strange moral arguments, as far as I can understand. If a killer has been very cool and calculating and mercenary about the murder and doesn't really feel bad about what he has done, then he says that they are a sort of type, a kind of person who will have no qualms about killing again because they have a warped moral code; they aren't insane, though. It's really interesting. I haven't done the article much justice.'

Melissa bit her lip. She was feeling uptight and sensitive. In her mind's eye every arrow pointed at her. It was as though she was wearing a luminous dress and the world was all black. She said, 'Are you getting at me, Steve?'

Steve stopped his tidying and stared at her incredulously. 'We're a bit sensitive today, aren't we Melissa?'

She frowned. 'Sod off.'

Steve sat down on the swivel chair by the till and moved around on it so that he faced Melissa directly. She was still staring out at the road with her back to him. He paused a while then said, 'I don't understand what's upset you so much all of a sudden, would you mind explaining?'

Melissa remained silent for a moment and then said, 'I feel like you're getting at me in some way. Like you're trying to make some kind of point. You've criticized me before for feeling and not acting, for not expressing myself and what I believe in with concrete acts. Maybe you think I'm a calculating person capable of really horrible things . . .'

Steve interrupted her, 'I've not said or implied anything of the sort. For God's sake Melissa, in your next breath you'll be accusing me of comparing you to Richard Gere.'

Melissa grunted and crossed her arms. 'Weren't you?'

Steve paused a moment and then said, 'Is something wrong with you today? Are you feeling ill?'

She shook her head.

'Well, what is it then?'

After a few seconds she turned from the doorway and faced him. Her eyes were tearful, 'I can't explain it. It's just that I feel so helpless and so furious inside at the same time.'

Steve frowned. 'Like frustrated?'

She shrugged again, 'I don't think so. I know it sounds stupid, but it's like I care about things so much and yet I don't seem to be able to do anything, like I'm frozen. Everything around me affects me so much, sad things cloud me up inside, I feel so terrible about homelessness and sadness and AIDS, loads of things, but I feel as though I can make no difference, I can't do anything to make things better. Nothing real, anyway.'

Steve looked mystified. He said, 'I just don't understand why it is that you feel compelled to feel bad about things all the time. It's so bland and aimless. It's like you've decided to feel bad just for the sake of it, just to look saintly and worthy. But you can't even be specific about your so-called sympathies. Just caring about things doesn't amount to much at the end of the day, it isn't enough.'

An incident popped into his head from a few weeks back in which he and Melissa had been walking home from a club in central London very early in the morning. He had been dressed up for a night out with his hair gelled and some make-up. As they waited at the bus stop a small group of men had approached him and taunted him: they had shouted in his face and abused him. The bus arrived in a minute or so and he had gladly climbed aboard before the situation turned violent. Throughout this incident Melissa had said and done nothing. He hadn't reprimanded her.

Melissa broke his reverie. 'It's not that I don't do anything, that isn't what matters. It's caring about things that matters. I do care about things.'

Steve stopped the music tape and changed it to something quieter and gentler. He knew that she was being sincere, but he still couldn't resist saying, 'Please cheer up, Melissa, we still have to work together you know.'

Melissa clammed up. They sat in silence for a few minutes. Steve flicked through his magazine some more, but couldn't concentrate. As a peace offering he said, 'Do you fancy some tea? I'm making.' Melissa shook her head sulkily. He made himself some tea and they sat in silence again. After a while he said, 'Why don't we cheer ourselves up with a bit of Power Selling?' He picked up a silver jacket which had a picture of the Last Supper on its back made entirely out of different coloured beads. 'You buy lunch if I sell this, OK?'

Melissa grimaced and marched off to make herself some coffee.

The next customer who came in was one of Steve's regulars. He had a good body and gregarious tastes. He liked Steve and he liked the jacket. By the time that Melissa had finished making her drink a deal had been transacted. He'd bought the jacket and they'd arranged to go out for a drink together after work. Once he'd left the shop, Steve couldn't resist saying, 'God, I'm hungry.'

Melissa stared at him coolly. 'I'm on a diet.'

Steve brushed a few tiny pieces of fluff from his tracksuit bottoms and ran a hand through his short, blond, bristly crew-cut. He said, 'I'm getting myself a Big Mac, all right?'

It was nearly three o'clock by the time John got home. As he shut the front door his arms ached on account of his having carried home a large, new toolbox complete with saws, chisels, a power drill and a small chain-saw. He put his new purchases down in the hallway and went and stood in his front room, scratching, stroking his stomach meditatively. He didn't have a garage; his front room would have to be as good as. He pushed his sofa up against a wall and dragged the two chairs into the hallway and then upstairs into his small bedroom. Next he got an old newspaper and used each page to wrap up various fragile glass and china objects before putting them into a box which he pushed into a corner of the room. He moved the bookcase into the hallway and pulled up the Turkish rug. He rolled it and leaned it up against the bookcase. The room was now much simpler and emptier. He dragged his new toolbox into the room and placed it in the middle of the floor, then opened it and arranged around it all the new things that he had bought so that he could inspect each item individually. He glanced at his watch, because he was waiting for a few deliveries. To pass the time while he waited he put on some plugs. Then he found a pencil, rubber, ruler and some paper and sat on the sofa making some initial, perfunctory plans. As his hand flew back and forth across the paper he felt the rest of his body relax, although the left-hand side of his anatomy was numb and heavy and his face was as pale and as puffy as dough.

On Wednesday morning Steve arrived slightly late at the shop. Melissa had already opened up by this time and was sat at the till organizing a float for the day. They still weren't speaking. All morning her chest had felt tight but empty at the same time. She knew that her body was making her suffer for the argument of the previous day. She knew inside that she had been self-indulgent and stupid, but she couldn't bring herself to say anything. This reticence was vindicated, however, when she turned as he entered the shop, a half-empty bag of coins still in her hand, and saw that he had a silver jacket slung casually over his shoulder. She tried to bite her tongue, but still said, 'I'd have thought that there would be easier ways of acquiring one of those jackets than that, Steve. Your little drink after work must've been quite successful – those things cost well over a hundred quid.'

Steve refused to be ruffled. He slung the jacket over the back of the swivel chair and said in a funny Oscar Wilde voice, 'Oh, I'm just borrowing it, darling. Everything has to be so tawdry and absolute in that little mind of yours. As it happens, he simply forgot his carrier bag in the pub last night and it seemed rather churlish of me to refuse to take possession of the coat until I see him again. I'm sure he'll be in later. Satisfied?'

She was satisfied but she didn't say anything. She felt bad. Steve made himself a cup of tea in silence and then slouched by the till and read his book. Melissa realized that he was punishing her, but this only made her feel more angry and defensive. She flicked through *Vogue* and said, 'Thanks for the tea.'

Steve looked at her for an instant. 'Grow up.'

He carried on reading. Melissa was determined to humiliate him, to turn the tables. She said, 'How about a game of Guess or Gush? At least if I win I'll get some tea. The next person we don't know who comes in, all right?'

Steve smiled to himself and said, 'Go ahead.'

Melissa smiled daggers back at him.

John's living-room floor was now awash with pieces of paper covered in complex sketches and plans, tools and electrical equipment, an unconstructed woodwork table which was at least seven feet long and four feet wide, and, up against one wall, four very large chunks of wood, beautiful pieces of half-tree with bits of shaggy bark still coating the outside, the inside glossy and luminous.

Accumulating his carpentry material had made John feel like a squirrel, a beaver, a humble creature compelled by the dictates of nature, by mortality, to build himself a secure nest, to build himself a coffin, to do-it-himself, to leave a mark, something self-created, something unique, individual and personal.

Instead of turning him away from death, his new involvement, his brand-new preoccupation had made him face death, had made him dive into the idea of death and swim around in it. Eventually he knew that it would drown him, but it didn't matter any more. He felt so vital.

It had been a wrench on Wednesday morning to drag himself away from his wood and his new tools and his schemes. Nevertheless, he had left for work at the usual time and had spent the morning at his desk phoning, making deals, securing sales. During his lunch-break he went out and bought a sandwich, then strolled around looking in shop windows.

Although everything felt very secure and normal to him again – his illness had been pushed away into a tiny crevice of his mind – he felt strangely light, as though luminated from within, powerful but weightless like a born-again Christian. His compulsion to buy, which had always been his guiding motivation, had, he felt, almost disappeared. He was fully aware of a deep irony in this situation, given that the previous day he had virtually emptied his savings account, but he now perceived those expenses as the beginning of something, and at the very same time as the end of something. He was cheerful in his hypocrisy and folly, like Don Quixote sitting backwards on his donkey, beguiled, foolish, happy.

He wandered into Soho, past the peepshows and then past some of the smarter and more expensive shops in the area. One shop window was based on an Aztec theme, full of gold and azure and orange. Everything was chunky and angular and sharp. The colours shouted out at him and he tried to picture in his mind an Aztec coffin made like a glorious offering to the sun god. He smiled to himself and resolved to get hold of some books on the subject as inspiration. The next shop window was based on a white theme. It was very clean and crisp, but ultimately uninspiring. John wanted to keep an open mind, however, so visualized a white-theme funeral with a white coffin lined in white satin with himself laid out inside in a Liberace suit of white and gold spangles. He liked the underlying implication of contradicting the blackness of death by offering himself in a clean white marriage to eternity, to eternal wedlock with nothingness, to space, to an infinite white silence.

Looking at his watch, John realized that it was almost the end of his lunch hour. He was just about to turn around when he caught sight of a young shorn-headed man standing in the doorway of the next shop along with a jacket slung over his arm. It was a silver jacket which was beautifully beaded on its back with some sort of colourful illustration. It looked silver and yet it wasn't a plastic or a leather jacket that had been spray-painted silver, it was a sort of soft, flickering silver velvet which shone and glistened like something organic. The young man was talking to someone who appeared to be a friend. He passed him the jacket and then gave him a peck on the cheek. His friend smiled, waved and then walked away. John waited a few seconds and then approached the young man before he'd had time to turn round and re-enter the shop. He smiled and said, 'Excuse me, would you tell me where you got the jacket that you were just holding?'

Steve smiled back at John, who seemed rather too middle-aged and tedious in his business suit to constitute a serious customer, 'That jacket comes from this shop. It's an original design so we only have a couple of them. Would you like to come in and see?'

John looked at his watch again and then thought, 'What the hell.'

He followed Steve into the shop. As he entered he noticed his helper giving a significant look to a girl who was standing leaning against the changing-room rail with a cigarette in her left hand and a copy of *Vogue* in her right. She looked up aggressively and then – somewhat surprisingly – immediately broke into a smile. John smiled back, but he kept his lips closed and his mouth formal. The young man said, 'I'm Steve, by the way. Hi.' He then sat down on a stool by the till and added, 'Melissa will serve you.'

Surprised at Steve's reticence to serve him John turned to the girl and said, 'I'm looking for a silver jacket like the one your friend . . .' He tipped his head in Steve's direction, but Steve was apparently already engrossed in what appeared to be *The Age of Reason*, '. . . the one like your friend just had over his arm outside the shop.'

Melissa's expression took on the trace of a slight sneer at the mention of the jacket. Vaguely uneasy, John added, 'If that's all right.' Then she smiled again. 'Sure, that's fine.'

She turned away and pulled a couple of hangers back to locate the item in question, then passed it to him. She said, 'Here you go. It's the last one we have, well, we only had two anyway. Nice fabric, isn't it?' John took hold of the jacket and ran his hand over the material, which was as soft as a peach. Melissa watched him for a moment and then said, 'Were you thinking of buying this for yourself?'

John realized that this must seem like a rather ridiculous proposition. He shook his head slowly. She said, 'I'm not surprised. It is rather, well, rather gaudy, isn't it?'

As Melissa said this she stared over his shoulder at Steve. She glared. John thought her strange and distracted. She made him feel ill-at-ease, with her bright clothes and short greased-back hair. He appreciated that he was under some obligation to explain his purpose, so he began to say, 'It's not so much the jacket I'm interested in as . . .'

Before he could finish his sentence, however, Melissa said, 'Hang on a sec,' and walked away from him over to the till, whereupon she snatched the book Steve was reading from his hand and picked up a pen. She turned to the title page and began to write with great vigour. Then she slammed the book down on the counter and returned to John's side.

Steve picked up his book looking highly disgruntled and irritated. He turned to the front page where Melissa had written in a large scrawl, THIS GUY IS SOME SORT OF MEDIA SALESMAN. I BET HE SELLS CRAP ON THE PHONE. HE'S GOT THAT SORT OF SMOOTH VOICE. EAT SHIT ARSEHOLE. Steve closed the book and placed it back down again.

On Melissa's return to his side John continued, 'It's not so much the jacket I'm interested in as the material.'

The girl's eyes were glassy and unfocused. She paused for a second and took a drag on her cigarette. 'What?'

John began to feel irritated. He said, 'I want to find out about the material, if that's not too much trouble.'

Melissa stared over at Steve and said, 'Steve can help you on this one.' She turned away and wandered to the back of the shop to fill the kettle in anticipation of her victory.

John was beginning to feel fairly disorientated. Steve stood up and strolled over to him saying, 'What was it you wanted?'

John was growing tired of repeating himself. He said, 'I want some of this material to line a coffin with.'

He expected the young man to show some surprise at this request, but instead he didn't appear to have listened and was now suddenly staring at John with what seemed to amount to a look of recognition. He then said, 'I don't mean to be nosy or anything, but don't you work in a media sales department. You know, selling stuff on the phone?'

John frowned. 'I said I wanted some of this material to line a coffin. Are you listening to me? What the hell do media sales have to do with anything?'

He was determined to possess some of the material that he held in his hand; it was as soft as tears, softer. Steve had the good sense to look slightly embarrassed. What the man was saying about coffins had just sunk in. He stared at John incredulously for a few seconds and then asked tentatively, 'May I ascertain from this that you are a coffin-maker?'

John appreciated the fact that this revelation must make him seem rather strange. The girl, Melissa, was staring at him with open-mouthed hostility. He thought, 'Maybe people don't like talking about death in high-fashion shops.'

He waited for a second and then said, 'Well I'm a sort of carpenter. I do things on commission, if you see what I mean. At the moment I happen to be making a coffin, yes.'

Steve began to smile at him. His face was very rosy and genuine when he smiled. He then said – rather inexplicably in John's opinion – 'God bless you!' and looked over at Melissa, 'Thirsty are we dear?' He started to laugh and went to sit down again; then picked up his book and ripped out the title page with great showiness. The girl looked very upset. John didn't know exactly what it was that he'd done to upset her but he presumed that it must be serious. She stalked towards him, took the coat and marched to the till. She said, 'I know the girl who designs these, I'll phone her and ask where she got the material from.' She dialled a number, smiling tremulously over her shoulder at John as she waited for an answer. She held on for a minute or so and then hung up. 'She isn't in, I'm afraid.'

John shrugged. He'd had enough. He said, 'It doesn't matter,' and turned to leave. But before he'd reached the door the girl was at his side and had rather inappropriately grabbed hold of his arm. She said, 'Don't go. I could try the number again.'

John was slightly shaken. He felt stupid and naïve. He felt disappointed too and oddly tearful. He pulled his arm away and said clumsily, 'What would you care anyway? Go back and read your stupid magazine.'

The girl seemed to freeze. She stared at him and suddenly her face was very simple and uncomplicated. She said, 'Have I upset you somehow? I really didn't mean to. I really do care.'

She said the last few words with especial emphasis. John blinked. His eyes felt ridiculously damp. She stared at him. He said, 'Your cigarette smoke got into my eyes. I'm allergic, that's all.'

She said again, 'I really do care. I'm sure that I could get hold of some of that material for you. I know I could. I promise.'

John shrugged helplessly. He didn't know what to do. Melissa was looking nervously around her and rubbing her nose in a gesture which seemed to express a mixture of both embarrassment and confusion. Then she said, 'I know, give me your phone number and when I get through to the designer I can phone you and tell you where she got her supply from.'

John pondered this idea for a moment, and placed his hand against the door frame for support. As he touched the painted wood his hand felt very cold. He could feel the wood but he couldn't properly feel it. His hand felt as though it had randomly been given a local anaesthetic. Surprisingly, his face and especially his tongue, felt very cold too. He blinked, realizing that these sensations had distracted him from the conversation at hand. Melissa was still staring at him. She looked confused. After a second she said, 'Are you all right? You don't look too well all of a sudden.'

John lied with surprising ease. His father had died of diabetes. He said, 'My blood-sugar levels get slightly low sometimes. This trip into town takes it out of me a bit. I didn't prepare for it. I'll get a taxi home, don't worry.'

His knees felt like cardboard, flimsy and thin. The doctor had said this would happen. It had happened before. He said again for emphasis, 'I'll get a taxi,' and turned. Unfortunately the words didn't come out this time as quickly as he'd anticipated. He'd turned before the first two syllables had been completed by his spongy and

132

ineffective tongue, and the force of his turn caused him to slam into the door frame. Melissa grabbed hold of his arm and said, 'Wait, I'll go and call one for you.'

She dashed out of the shop and ran to the top of the road and on to a busier street, where she tried to hail a cab.

Steve approached John's gradually collapsing form and, putting his arm around his waist, pulled him down into a sitting position. He sat by him on the step. He said softly, 'Can you say your address?' John nodded, humiliated, and started to mumble. Steve got up and went to the till where he grabbed a pen and the first bit of paper that came to hand, then he returned to John's side and patted his arm as he said, 'Go on then, slowly.'

Breathing deeply, John gradually formed each word. It took an immense effort. He felt very tired, and his eyes kept blinking.

In a couple of minutes Melissa returned to the shop with a taxi in tow. When she saw John slumped on the step she felt intensely sorry for him. Steve said, 'Come and help him up at the other side. I don't know whether we shouldn't send him to hospital.'

John shook his head violently at this suggestion. He drawled, 'I'm fine. I'm fine.'

Together they lifted him up and eased him into the taxi. John helped as best he could although he felt very drowsy and ineffectual. Melissa said, 'Maybe I should go home with him, Steve?'

John said, 'No, I'm fine!' as emphatically as he could, putting out one of his hands in the gesture a traffic warden might use to stop oncoming traffic: palm flat, arm outstretched. Steve handed the taxi driver the paper that he'd written the address on and said, 'Are you sure that you've got the money to pay for this taxi?'

John nodded very determinedly although his eyes were closed, and patted at his jacket where his inside pocket was located with a floppy hand. He said, 'I'm fine,' and waved sloppily. Steve slammed the door shut and thanked the taxi driver. He also added by way of explanation, 'Don't worry, he's not drunk, he's a diabetic.' The taxi driver nodded and answered cheerily, 'I don't mind what he is so long as he doesn't smoke or vomit.' He then performed a three-point turn and sped away.

Melissa and Steve stood together on the pavement watching the taxi disappearing into the traffic at the top of the road. Steve said, 'God, I really feel bad about this. We've been so fucking insensitive and awful. Maybe it's our fault.'

Melissa had entirely forgotten that she was angry with him. She wiped the corners of her mouth furtively with her first finger and thumb to ensure that her red lipstick hadn't bled or smudged in all the excitement. Then she stared at him with her deep brown eyes and said, 'What do you mean? I said I'd get him some material and I will.' Steve snorted, 'It's not the bloody material that's the issue here, Melissa, it's the way we both behaved. We must've seemed really rude. We obviously confused and distressed him. We upset him and I think that's why he got ill.'

Melissa looked bemused. She said, 'What are you talking about, Steve? We were only having a bit of fun. He wanted some material and I phoned for him, which is more than most people would've done.'

Steve felt helpless and furious. He looked into Melissa's eyes and frowned. 'I can't work out if you're just stupid or if you're simply insensitive. I think the scales are weighed quite heavily in both directions.'

She smiled humourlessly, 'That's an appropriate image. I'm a Gemini.'

Steve turned his back on her and re-entered the shop. Eventually Melissa followed him in. He had made himself a cup of tea and was talking on the phone. After a few seconds he hung up and said, 'I was getting that guy's phone number while I still have his address in mind.' He had written John's address and phone number down on a till receipt in tiny writing. Melissa frowned. 'What are you doing that for?' Steve shrugged, 'So I can phone him when I've got some information on the material. Anyway, I think that it'd be nice to know that he was OK.'

Melissa slammed her hand down hard on the top of the till and said, 'I didn't mean "what are you doing that for?", I meant "what are *you* doing that for?" He's my customer, I'll deal with him over the phone.' Steve laughed nastily. He said, 'It's a bit late to be getting all possessive, don't you think? You've already said outside that you don't give a shit; well I do.'

Melissa's face was angry and blotchy. 'I said no such thing! Of course I'm concerned. I said I'd get him the material and I will.'

Steve grabbed his tracksuit jacket which was slung over the back of the chair. He put it on and half-zipped it up. As he walked to the door he said, 'I'm going out for a walk and to get some lunch. Can you manage alone while I'm out?'

Melissa had picked up the till receipt and was studying it. 'Of course I can. I think I'll try and phone again while you're gone.'

He didn't bother responding.

John remembered very little about getting home. When he awoke he felt as though he had been asleep for several hours, but when he looked at his watch it was only twenty past two. His lunch break had formally ended about an hour earlier. He was stretched out on his living-room sofa, cushioned by numerous pieces of paper. Under his shoulder were a couple of pencils and a ruler. He chucked them on to the floor with one hand and arranged himself more comfortably. His body felt stiff and tight. He shut his eyes for a while and rested. Inside he felt bad about not returning to work. Usually he was extremely responsible and reliable. He debated the possibility of returning into town but then decided that in his present condition it might be more sensible for him to phone in and explain his relapse.

Slowly he sat up and swung his legs on to the floor. He still felt weak. His hands were clenched into tight white-knuckled balls, and he endeavoured to clench them harder, as though these fists would generate power and momentum. He reached groggily for the telephone which he had put on the floor next to the sofa the previous day when he'd been rearranging things. He picked it up and phoned work. It only took a second. He spoke to one of the receptionists. The hand that he'd used to dial was still closed, except for the finger which he'd used to press the buttons. As he made his excuses he studied this hand. Although it remained slightly numb he was still capable of feeling the sharp sensation of a ball of paper crumpled up inside the fleshy palm of his fist. He opened up his hand and inspected it. It was the page of a book, a torn out leaf. On one side he saw his address. On the other side, written in a large messy scrawl, were the words THIS GUY IS SOME KIND OF MEDIA SALESMAN. I BET HE SELLS CRAP ON THE PHONE. HE'S GOT THAT SORT OF SMOOTH VOICE. EAT SHIT ARSEHOLE. John pondered the meaning of this for a few seconds after he'd put the telephone receiver back down. Gradually Melissa's face – a blurred cartoon characterization of it with blood-red lips and hair dripping in oil, slicked back like Dracula's – returned to his memory. He remembered her writing something down on the front page of a book. It confused him though. He lay back down on his side and re-read it. It was clear to him that what she had written was a description of himself, but he failed to understand her motivation. All that seemed feasible was that the two of them had had a bet on or were playing a game. He relaxed his head and looked sideways at the ceiling. He thought, 'It doesn't really matter why she wrote those things, the terrible thing is that she did write them. In a matter of minutes, in the shortest of exchanges, she managed to discover with perfect accuracy the details of my life. I must be as transparent as an amoeba under a microscope, a walking, talking, living, breathing telesales man; nothing more. I may feel inside that I am more significant than that, that I amount to more, but I don't.'

He thought of what she had written again. THIS GUY IS A NOBODY, HE SELLS CRAP ON THE TELEPHONE, HE HAS A SMOOTH VOICE. HE IS A PHONY. THE WORLD WILL TURN WITHOUT HIM. 'God!' he thought, 'I'm so dispensable. I'm so insignificant.'

The telephone started ringing. He sat up and reached out for it, grasped it in his hands and jerked it violently away from its connection in the wall. Its slim plug slipped out of its socket. It stopped ringing. In the new silence he threw the telephone at the wall several times and was struck with wonderment at its hardiness. He resolved that during the remainder of his life the telephone would be an anathema. That chapter was closed.

When Steve returned from his lunch hour Melissa was serving a couple of customers. After they had gone he said, 'Did you get through?' Melissa shook her head. 'It was a bit odd. It appeared to ring for a short while and then the tone switched to disconnected. I phoned the operator and she said that the number was temporarily unobtainable.'

Steve sighed. 'Maybe try again later. I suppose you gave it your best shot.'

Melissa smiled. 'Can I gather that we are now friends again? You don't seem as uptight with me as earlier.'

He smiled back. 'I'll make some tea.'

As he pottered around at the rear of the shop, filling the kettle from their tiny sink and plugging it into the wall, she said, 'I made a decision while you were gone, by the way.'

Steve frowned. 'What sort of decision?'

She squatted next to him as he put a couple of tea bags into mugs which were balanced on the tray with the kettle, and said, 'Well, I got through to Stephanie on the phone and she said that she bought that fabric at the Material Centre down on Berwick Street. So after work I'm going to go and buy a length and then tomorrow I'll take it around to his place.'

Steve shook his head as he stirred the tea and grasped the tired, boiled bags in two tentative fingers before tossing them into the bin. 'Firstly, it'll cost you a fortune, secondly, how will you know what quantity to buy? Thirdly, don't you think it's a bit risky going around to the house of a strange man who you've hardly met before?'

All these things were true. Melissa shrugged and said, 'Forget about it, OK?'

John spent the afternoon building his work-bench. Intense physical activity was probably best avoided in his present condition – he'd never been a physical person and although he'd always been naturally skinny and relatively well-proportioned, the closest he ever came to regular exercise was an occasional swim – but building the work-bench seemed an excellent initiation into the world of carpentry. It was also a necessary distraction. He felt very depressed.

When he'd completed the bench he stared around the room for a moment and contemplated his new pile of tools, then tried to organize them into a neat and tidy display against one of the walls so that they wouldn't get lost or broken as he worked. When everything was arranged he grasped a large chunk of wood and dragged it on to the work-bench. It was extraordinarily heavy. He took his new plane and slid it back and forth over the surface of the wood. Initially the thick bark came away, then paler shavings curled away from the wood with almost erotic precision. They were so thin and delicate. After a few seconds he stopped and picked up a handful. He sniffed them and they smelled like a cageful of school gerbils, musty but clean. Dropping the shavings, he went and sat down on the sofa again. He pulled at his shirt collar; he was still wearing his office clothes although he had removed his jacket and tie and had rolled up his sleeves. He rubbed his eyes, which felt sore, and picked up a few of the coffin designs that he'd made the previous evening. Some included very ornate side-panelling and lids which were intricately carved. He put these aside; they seemed rather ambitious. His coffin had to be a practical proposition, not a dream. He had to face the fact that his time for construction would be limited and as a reflection of this new practical realism, to curtail his more extravagant and fanciful notions.

After a while he went into his hallway and squatted next to his bookcase where he pulled out a few of the coffee-table art books that he had managed to accumulate over the years but which he had actually never read. He carried five back into the living room and sat down to peruse them.

As he paged through them he sensed the downy silence in the house, a quiet interrupted only by the brutal slicing sound of the turning pages. He had carried his television upstairs when he was building his bench because space had suddenly been reduced to a minimum. He went into the kitchen and picked up his little portable radio which he listened to in the morning while making breakfast, and carried it through to the living room where he balanced it on top of the mantelpiece, and tuned to Radio One. He felt as though he needed the blare of chat and music to lift him up and propel him into the world of physical labour; the challenge of practical creation. He returned to the sofa and his design books. Nothing immediately took his fancy. Although he liked much of what he saw, very little seemed appropriate for a coffin. Coffins were, after all, rather formal in design. Boxes.

He entertained the idea of a coffin that was merely simple and brightly painted, but that wasn't quite enough. He entertained the notion of a theme coffin, something based on Picasso's blue period for example or maybe even a Cubist coffin. If he had a Cubist coffin he decided that it wouldn't have to be a straight box. Instead he would build it so that it moved in an angular curve, and his body would be laid out inside it in a comfortable banana shape.

After considerable thought, however, he was forced to face the possibility that his body might not be very pliable in death and that this arrangement might not show him off to his best advantage. He didn't want his body to look as though it had merely been jammed into his coffin at a convenient angle. The formality of death necessarily involved the body being layed out in a specific way, and he had no real desire to flout this tradition. He had never guarded a secret desire to be buried face-down, for example, in a coffin like a cheese dish.

The very idea of a coffin was, he supposed, to display the body at its best in a deathly repose. He thought, 'The coffin is, after all, about the body. The body is what gives it meaning, no matter what ideas have been generated over the centuries about the coffin as an independent entity, its only simple and necessary function is as a display case. It is also like a file which holds in papers and keeps them in order. It is a limited space which, practically speaking, is on a par with a yoghurt carton or a can of beans.'

He immediately threw down the book he was looking at and picked up another from the pile. He flicked through its pages very rapidly until he found what he was looking for and then stared at it with great fixity for several minutes. Then he repeated quietly to himself, 'It's a limited and very practical space which, to all intents and purposes makes it just the same as a yoghurt carton or a can of beans.'

What about a can of soup? He returned his gaze once more to the Warhol print and debated how difficult it would be to make a coffin that was shaped like an old-style Campbell's can. Obviously there would be practical difficulties, especially given that he had had very little practice at carpentry over the last twenty odd years.

He impulsively began to roll down his sleeves as though preparing to smarten himself up to go out, but as he fastened his first cuff it occurred to him that after his earlier difficulties it would be inadvisable to venture out in case he felt unwell again or over-exerted himself. Although he was now intensely keen to get some appropriate books on practical woodwork – creating a surface that was perfectly curved or circular was going to be highly problematic – he decided instead to spend the early evening composing a letter of resignation for work and preparing a small meal. He felt quite hungry.

It was just after four o'clock on Thursday afternoon when Melissa stepped out of Mile End tube station and into the rain. She was carrying a large carrier bag full of material, which she held close against her body so that it would keep as dry as possible. That morning she had inspected an *A to Z* so that she would know which direction to head off in.

She walked for several minutes, becoming increasingly damp even though she wore a bright yellow transparent raincoat which was covered in a design of brash white daisies. The raincoat was, it appeared, more fashionable than practical.

Eventually she was able to locate the correct road and then the right house. It was a small place made out of old red brick which had grown dark and dirty over the years because of London smoke and exhaust fumes. It looked in its simplicity every bit like a drawing that a young child might make of a house, with four small windows and a door almost in the middle; except that this house was not alone in a garden with a tree and an outsize sun, but was flanked on either side by identical houses which ran off down the road like different sections of a long centipede.

It was a dull afternoon, so inside the house the lights were on downstairs. Melissa uttered a sigh of relief. On the tube she had worried that he would be out and that she would be forced to call again. Drawing up close to the door, she put out a wet hand and rang the bell.

John was busy in his living-room tacking a series of woodwork-made-simple illustrations on to the wall. Next to these were a selection of illustrations of Warhol's work, and of course, centrally positioned, an illustration of his Campbell's soup cans. These he had enlarged on a photocopier earlier that day.

That morning John had been out shopping. He had bought a comprehensive selection of brushes and paints which he had selected with painstaking attention to colour.

His entire body shuddered when the doorbell rang. He wasn't expecting a call and he had no desire to see anyone. He felt like a tiny sea mussel which was snug and moist inside its charcoal shell, waiting for the sea and yet not waiting, independent, serene.

The doorbell rang again. He pushed the last pin into the wall and then hurried to answer it. When he opened it his immediate thoughts were, 'Who is she, and what the hell is she doing here?'

Melissa could barely recognize the man she had spoken to the day before. He looked entirely different. He seemed a lot thinner and younger out of his suit. His brown hair was obviously unbrushed and his face seemed worn and wary. This effect – she decided – might have been exacerbated by the slight shadow of a beard that he had grown overnight.

After he had opened the door he stared at her for a moment and touched his chin with his hand. She said, 'Hello. I don't expect that you'll remember me but I was at the shop yesterday when . . .' – she paused for a moment – '. . . when you wanted to buy some material.' He frowned and rubbed his chin some more. She added, 'I'm sorry if I've interrupted you but I've got some of the material that you wanted.' She indicated the bag with a slight movement of her head. He said, 'I haven't shaved today,' and before she could reply he added, 'but then why the hell should I? I'm my own boss.'

In his mind he thought of the incident on Charing Cross Road a couple of days before and smiled to himself. Then he reached out his hands towards the bag she was holding. 'Let me take that from you. I suppose the least I could do is offer you a hot drink. It's very wet.'

Melissa wasn't sure whether it was sensible to follow him in, especially after Steve's warning on the previous day, but she was cold and damp. To cover herself she said pointedly, 'Steve would have come but he's busy at the shop. He sends his best wishes.' Then she followed him in and closed the door behind her.

John walked through the hallway and into the kitchen. In the living room the radio was spilling out the top twenty at full volume. He switched on the kettle with one hand and then reached inside the bag that she had brought and whistled. 'How did you guess what sort of amount I'd need?'

She shrugged and this movement tipped a hundred tiny raindrops snailing down her mac. 'Well, I thought it'd need to be quite wide and very long if it was for a coffin. I didn't know whether you'd line the lid as well so I got extra.'

He looked at her sharply. 'Good point.'

He hadn't got round to considering this yet himself. Then he said uncomfortably, 'I'd forgotten that I'd mentioned that it was for my . . .' – he paused – '. . . the coffin.'

She looked past him and towards the kettle, from which steam was now emerging, 'Yes, you did. Do you mind if I take my mac off? I'm a bit damp.'

He reached out a hand for the mac, slung it over the draining board and then removed two mugs from underneath it with one hand. She said, 'Let me take the material and get it out of harm's way. You don't want to spill coffee on it or get it wet.'

He gave her the bag and said, 'Put it on the sofa in the living room. I'll bring the coffee through.'

She nodded. 'Milk, no sugar please,' and moved off in the direction he'd indicated.

John switched off the kettle and made the coffee. He felt jittery and nervous. He was embarrassed by the idea of having a strange woman in his home, but was even more uneasy when he considered the scrawled message that he'd accidentally acquired the previous day. Suddenly it was very important to him that she should not think that she could see through him again. He was determined to be something more than what she had seen the day before, to create a new life out of nothing for himself before he died, to become something significant, something exceptional and extraordinary. He picked up the coffee cups and padded into the living room.

Melissa was sitting on the sofa paging through one of his coffee-table design books. She had turned the radio off. She looked up, smiled and reached out her hand for the coffee. He tried not to spill any when he passed it to her. She said, 'You've got a weird set-up here. A lot of the young designers that I know work from home. Have you only just got started?'

He shook his head quickly. 'No. Well, yes. I used to work for someone else and now I've set up on my own. This is one of my first private commissions, so it's all a bit perfunctory.'

She smiled. 'That shows great initiative.'

He tried not to let her patronizing tone affect his expression. She frowned. 'I didn't mean that to sound patronizing. I suppose I'm just a bit jealous. I'd love to have the nerve to do something like this; you know, to be independent and creative. I don't really have the gumption.' She paused and then said, 'I made this shirt I'm wearing myself.' He studied the shirt. It was rather unusual but well-tailored in a purple silky material. He said, 'It's nice.' She shrugged and sipped her coffee.

He felt slightly strange talking about someone else for a change, given that his thoughts had become so charged and introspective over the past few days. He relaxed. 'No, I mean it. It's very stylish. It's just as smart as anything that you see in the shops. It's certainly a lot better made than most stuff you can buy.'

She smiled. He could see by the confidence in her eyes that he had won her over. She was now at her ease and believed the entire situation to be as it seemed. She said, 'I can't deny that I was surprised when you said that you made coffins the other day.'

He leaned against the work-bench and warmed his hands on his cup. 'Oh yeah? Didn't I fit neatly into whatever categorizations you have for carpenters or coffin makers?'

She shook her head and had the good grace to appear embarrassed. 'Maybe I should be honest about this.'

He raised his eyebrows – he hoped encouragingly – and she continued, 'Well, we play a lot of silly jokes in the shop, otherwise we get bored. Steve had dared me that I wouldn't be able to guess the profession of the next person who came into the shop. I know this sounds silly. The next person that came into the shop who I didn't already know was, well, was you and I thought on first impressions that you were a salesman or something. You have a very smooth, confident voice.'

John smiled. 'But you were wrong.'

She smiled back. 'I guess so.'

After a few seconds John put his coffee cup down and picked up the bag of material from the sofa. He touched it again and said, 'If I was going to sleep for ever I'd want this softness to surround me. It's incredible.'

Melissa nodded. She said warmly, 'I'm really keen to know what you are intending to do with it.'

He suddenly felt very shy. 'It's not all that interesting.' He loved the feel of the material but hadn't really fitted it as yet into the great scheme of things. He stared at it for a moment, then his heart lifted and he said, 'In fact this is quite incredible. Yesterday when I saw this material I didn't really have the first clue about what design I was going to use for this piece. I was just drawn to it because it was gorgeous. But last night I made a few plans without even considering this fabric as a part of the scheme, and believe it or not, it fits in perfectly. It's fantastic!'

He walked over to his drawings and illustrations on the wall. 'In my design I'm attempting to create something unusual and beautiful that is both about the physical and . . .' he paused, '. . . the metaphysical.' She frowned, 'I don't get it.'

He thought for a moment and then ran one of his hands through his hair, slicking it back and pulling out some of the tangles. Then he stopped what he was doing and held out his hand to her and wiggled his fingers, 'What's this?'

She stared at him incredulously. 'It's your hand.'

He nodded. 'Right, it's my hand, but it has the capacity to be many things. Just now I used it as a comb. My separate fingers were individual spokes, each one brushing my hair into place.' He picked up his coffee and tipped a small amount into his cupped palm. Some of it dribbled down his arm. The coffee was still very hot, but he didn't seem to feel it. He said, 'What is it now?'

She shrugged. 'Is it a cup? Or a bowl?'

He nodded. 'That's it! That's the idea. Well, what I want to do with my coffin design is the same sort of thing. The design has a physical aspect – it encloses a body, a dead body – but it also has another purpose, a purpose beyond its practical use.'

She frowned again. 'Like what? Like to look attractive, or what?'

He smiled, exhilarated, 'Yes, to look attractive, but also to be ironic, to point back at itself and say "So much has been said about death, but this is a parody of death, makes light of death, makes death into something concrete and individual."'

He paused for a moment. 'I'm not making much sense, am I?'

She grimaced. 'Ever so slightly. Maybe it's possible to make comparisons in the worlds of art or fashion. In our shop the clothes we make and sell are very extrovert and unusual. A lot of them are impractical, loud, brash, silly. People have to be very adventurous to wear them; flashy, I suppose. In many ways though, the clothes really make fun of themselves, make fun of fashion. They *are* fashionable, yet they are individual. They are extreme. They take designs and shapes that other people might wear and they exaggerate them, make fun of them, they take everything to the extreme, to the point at which they become totally silly and impractical.'

She stopped. 'I'm talking nonsense.'

He laughed. 'We both are.'

While she had been talking he had been sipping the coffee out of his palm. His hand was now wet and he wiped it on his trousers. 'I tell you what. I've got a bottle of wine in the kitchen, do you want to share it? I feel like a drink.'

Although somewhat surprised by his sudden sociability, Melissa nodded her head keenly – 'I'd love to' – and watched him as he left the room and then listened to his various clatterings out in the kitchen. He returned with an open bottle of red and two glasses. As he poured he said, 'When you think about the sort of fashion that your shop promotes you have to think about the fact that you are fashion leaders. Fashion always starts off with extreme ideas which are eventually modified into the mainstream.'

Melissa nodded and stood up to get her glass of wine, 'I suppose coffins – the idea of them – hasn't been very controversial for a good while.'

He took a sip of his wine and grimaced. 'I suppose not. But if you think back to the time when tombs in churches were designed to be as showy as possible, when small amounts of wealth and fame were sufficient justification for a life-sized stone sculpture of the person attached to the lid of the stone coffin . . . I suppose in those instances though the idea of the coffin as a box and the headstone as a spectacle had become enmeshed.'

Melissa said quickly, 'Yes, but think about the Egyptians for example. I remember the big Tutankhamen exhibition from when I was a tiny kid – with all those great gold and enamel sarcophaguses – they probably took coffin design as far as it's possible to go.'

John nodded his agreement and leaned against his woodwork table again. 'What I want to do is in many ways a contradiction of that extravagance and that idealization of death. By being excessive I almost feel as though those tomb-makers were in a stage of denial. They wanted to deny the fact that death changes everything. They wanted things to remain as before.'

As he spoke he stared into Melissa's eyes, which seemed very lively. She was grinning vivaciously.

'Maybe you think I'm talking rubbish? This is all really just off the top of my head.'

Her grin diminished slightly, 'No, I think it's fascinating. Do you give as much thought to all the pieces you make?'

John felt momentarily restricted. 'I believe in giving my all, however much that amounts to. In many ways I suppose that the idea is the most important thing. Once you've thought about something, taken a stance, made plans, that's half the battle won.'

Melissa's smile returned. She said, 'I know exactly what you mean there. It's like a commitment, a state of mind. Sometimes that's all that matters. It's like goodwill.'

John frowned slightly and walked over to add an extra tack to the corner of one of his pictures on the wall, 'Well, it's more like an intention really, a decision to act, to change things mentally so that they are changed in fact; a tiny alteration of mental perspective and the whole world is different.'

They stared at each other for a moment, both confused. Melissa quickly looked at her watch and then drained her glass, 'I think I'd probably better get going before I hit the rush hour on the tube. I live quite a good way away.'

John nodded. 'I've enjoyed meeting you again. I really must repay you for that material. I bet it cost a fortune.'

As he spoke he disappeared from the room and returned holding her damp mac. Melissa stood up and took it from him. She said, 'It wasn't cheap. The receipt's in the bag.'

He found it and took out his wallet, giving her a couple of notes. He said, 'You can't imagine how grateful I am. It's been great chatting to you, a real distraction. You've really helped me to crystallize my thoughts. I feel all focused and purposeful!'

Melissa smiled and put on her coat. She said, 'I'd love to pop round again and see how it's going, even though I haven't quite clarified in my mind what on earth it is that you're intending to do.'

John escorted her to the door. 'Come any time. I'd really like you to drop by again. Thanks for everything.'

He opened the door for her. His face ached from smiling. Melissa turned and waved goodbye. After he'd closed the door, John leant against it and held on to the handle. He closed his eyes and his face shone with sweat.

The following day, Steve wanted to know all about the previous afternoon. When Melissa arrived in the morning she had a great air of self-satisfaction and smugness. She was wearing a dress that she had designed and made herself which he had not seen before. He slouched against the changing room curtains and appraised her as she took off her coat and checked her make-up. 'That's a new frock. Nice. How did it go yesterday?'

Melissa smiled. 'I made this myself. It went well. He's a really nice guy, strange but nice. We had a good chat.'

Steve grinned, 'What about, the art of coffin-making?'

Melissa shrugged, 'Joke if you want. There's a lot more to him than meets the eye.'

Steve stopped grinning and began to look interested. He said incredulously, 'You didn't get off with him?'

Melissa squealed, 'Of course I bloody didn't. It's not like that.'

'Well, what is it like?' he interrupted.

She looked sceptical and remote, 'It's none of your business, Steve, it's private. Anyway, I'd feel silly telling you, I think you'd laugh at me.'

He tried to stop looking frivolous and lowered his voice in an attempt at sincerity. 'Go on, tell me. Of course I won't make fun of you. I'm really interested.'

She paused a moment and then fiddled for a second with the hem on her dress. 'Well, it's like, . . . I don't know . . . it's like we've got so much in common. It's sort of an attitude of mind, a creative sincerity, an intensity. It's like we're very similar as people. We want the same things. He made me feel inspired.'

Steve watched her very closely and then said, 'Be honest, do you fancy the guy?'

She shook her head, 'No, I don't, he's nice but that's all. It's more than that. It's like we think in the same way. He says a lot of things that really reflect how I feel. He's really interesting.'

Someone came into the shop and browsed around. As he kept an eye on them Steve said quietly, 'Are you going to see him again then?' She nodded. 'Eventually.' Then she picked up her copy of *Vogue*.

That morning John stayed in bed until ten. The previous night he'd worked without pause until the early hours and he awoke feeling worn and drained. Since the beginning of his illness he'd found the start of the day increasingly arduous and impossible. Nevertheless, on awakening he struggled up and slung on the previous day's clothes – which were ingrained with saw-dust and grime – and set off downstairs to make some tea and to get work underway.

The previous evening he'd negotiated the intricate process of creating a smooth circular shape out of one of his big blocks; a perfect curve to mirror the crude curve of the wood but more exact, man-made. It had been a complicated and painstaking procedure but already he was making progress and was optimistic.

He'd had to measure himself very precisely (it felt morbid) so that he could make sure that the coffin was as short and compact as possible. He wanted to create a box which was realistically tin-shaped, a practical length and not too wide. He realized that there were likely to be restrictions on size when it came to coffins in terms of burial space. To make it too broad would be inadvisable.

He was still thinking about the lid. Initially he had been keen to have a hinged door on the coffin, probably following along the edge of the label, which would open up like a car door to reveal his body within. Eventually, however, he'd been forced to acknowledge the fact that this design was too complicated to construct and also that it would make keeping the size to a minimum and fitting the body – his body – into the coffin through a slightly more restricted space problematic. He supposed that it would be possible to push and slide the body into the coffin head-first, but felt that this would be a bit inelegant and undignified.

Instead, therefore, he opted for a classical coffin lid design; although the lid would not hang over the base of the coffin, it would fit together with the base, leaving barely a hint as to where the actual join was; like one of those brightly painted Russian dolls which smoothly opens to reveal several others inside, each smaller than the other but all intrinsically identical.

John pursued realism in his design like a bloodhound on a scent. He wanted his tin, his coffin, to look like an original Campbell's soup can but also to look like Warhol's paintings of the cans. The difference was subtle but significant. The beautiful silver material that Melissa had brought him would line the can, the coffin, and it would be a legitimate colour, have an appropriate sheen for the inside of a tin; enclosing him, preserving him like a product, a foodstuff for worms. A can of decay.

As he worked he smiled grimly at the notion of placing a sell-by date on the top half of the tin, something like BEST BEFORE FIRST MONTH OF INTERNMENT. He imagined people excavating his coffin in hundreds of years' time and studying it, finding meaning where he had intended it to be; maybe even more meaning than he was capable of understanding at this juncture, from his own limited perspective, caught in the moment of creation as he was, restricted by his time to only understanding so much. He revitalized himself by thinking, 'This thing I am creating has more meaning than even I can understand'.

During the following week John left the house only once, and that was to go to Safeways for some provisions and to a hardware store to buy wood tacks, nails and a wood file. He also bought glue. The rest of the time he stayed inside and listened to the radio, worked solidly and took to sleeping at night on the sofa downstairs. He wanted to conserve his energy, which was at a minimum, like a coin-fed gas meter at its lowest ebb, ready to run out, to close down.

Melissa was very sunny at work and busy with life. She looked forward to seeing John again but wanted a dignified period to pass before she pestered him. Her next visit was on a Saturday afternoon. Steve had agreed to cover for her if she went home early from work. She said she wanted to buy more material for her clothes designs. In fact she went straight to an off licence to buy some wine, then down to the tube.

John took a good while to answer the door. During the previous week or so this had been his technique for getting rid of frivolous callers. There had only been a couple.

He had thought about Melissa a great deal over the past eight or nine days, not romantically, although had he been anticipating staying alive for more than the shortest of periods he would almost definitely have attempted to view her in such a light. In his state of violent activity he thought of her in terms of a confidante, an inspirationee, someone he could revitalize with his last dregs of energy.

When he opened the door he smiled widely and said, 'It's great to see you again, come in!'

Melissa was shocked to see how different he looked. He appeared to be much thinner, more gaunt, but his face was now hidden by the beginnings of a red-tinged shaggy beard. His eyes were grey and his clothes were terribly unkempt. There seemed to be a fine pale sheen that covered him from head to foot; after a moment she realized that this must be a million tiny specks of sawdust.

John noticed her expression and said at once, 'I know that I look a mess, it's just that I get very involved in what I do. I'm driven. I don't seem to have much energy for anything else.'

She followed him in and said, 'You do look a bit like the Wild Man of Borneo.'

He smiled and took the wine that she offered on the way through to the kitchen.

No washing-up had been done since her last visit. Everything was dirty, everything had a sawdust sheen. She said, 'Do you have any clean glasses?'

He ran a tap and washed a couple. 'I'm sorry about this. I've been really busy.'

Melissa found a bottle-opener and pulled out the cork. He shook the glasses dry – she was relieved that he didn't use one of the dusty tea-towels available – and she poured in some wine. She said, 'I'm glad you were in. It looks like you haven't left the place since last week. Have you achieved much?'

He took a sip of wine and smiled as he sighed with gratification. 'I've done so much that I feel bloody reborn. I can't explain it, I feel so gratified. It's like magic the way that things just slot together. If they don't work out you just have to try again, focus all your attention, find endless patience and eventually you attain your goal, no matter how tiny it is. You put in a nail straight or you file something into a perfect curve, make a join that is faultless. It's fantastic.'

As he spoke he used his hands like descriptive tools. Melissa

151

hadn't noticed this before. He looked like Michelangelo to her. She almost felt jealous, he was so much like a child. She said, 'I can't believe your enthusiasm. If I were you I'd collapse from exhaustion if I got so excited about every dress that I made. Do you treat every piece like a first?'

His eyes slitted slightly and he rubbed at his nose with the hand not holding his wine glass. 'Everything in life is a conquest. Each thing is different. At this moment I believe I'd feel the same excitement in my gut even if I were fifty years older and creating this object for the hundredth time. I feel the sort of sense of achievement that comes from doing something well. That's enough. It's enough for me anyway, like a physical empathy with objects. It's like I'm God and I've created a perfect tree or a perfect river. It's like I now understand what makes the world tick.'

She couldn't resist laughing at him. He stared at her, his expression one of surprise.

Eventually she said, 'You sound so naïve. It's really funny. Refreshing too I suppose, but funny.'

He led her into the living room. Before she entered the room she glanced towards the front door again and said. 'Why haven't you opened any of the letters on your doormat? There's a whole pile of them.'

He shrugged. 'No point. I'm too busy. Forget about them.'

She followed him into the living room and looked around in amazement. The floor was inches deep in chips, slivers, specks and flakes of wood. She said, 'When I was a kid I had a hamster and it lived in a place like this.' She felt she was going to sneeze. 'Doesn't this stuff get up your nose? Surely you wear a mask while you work? This fine dust could destroy your lungs.'

'I can't be bothered.' He grimaced, then ran his hand down the base of the coffin, which was now complete, like a big round canoe with flat ends. He looked up at her. 'What do you think?'

She frowned. 'Explain it to me. It seems a strange shape for a coffin.'

He smiled. 'Remember when we were chatting last time and I said that I wanted to make something which had a meaning beyond its purpose? Something which satirized death, brought it down to earth and yet celebrated it? Well that's what this is, that's what this shape means.'

Melissa interrupted him. 'Has someone commissioned this then? They must be very weird. I bet it'll cost them a fortune.'

This put John off his stroke. He sipped his wine, 'Yes, it's been commissioned. It's for someone who . . .'

He paused. 'It won't be too expensive.'

Melissa put out her hand and touched the wood. 'God, it feels really smooth, no splinters or anything.'

He said, 'I want it to feel as smooth as steel, smooth and cold.'

Melissa ran her hand around the inside. 'Well, why didn't you make it out of steel then?'

He laughed, frustrated. 'Because it's a coffin, stupid. Coffins are made out of wood, that's the whole point of them. This is a coffin. It will look like something else, it will have an appearance to the contrary, but it will still, intrinsically, be a coffin.'

She took her hand from the coffin and blew away the fine dust which had accumulated on the tips of her fingers, 'So how will it look? What will it be, apart from a coffin, that is?'

John pointed towards the pictures that he'd tacked to the wall, many of which were now rather bedraggled and dog-eared. 'It will look like a silver can, a tin, a container. I'm using Warhol's ideas but taking them further. He made art from everyday objects. I'm doing the same thing but my art is functional.'

Melissa frowned and chewed the corner of her bottom lip for a while. 'You mean that this coffin is going to look like one of those Campbell's cans? That's strange.'

John shrugged defensively. 'It's no stranger in real terms than the outfit which you are wearing today. How is this different?'

Melissa was wearing a pair of flared tartan trousers and a pink turtleneck top with bell-shaped sleeves. Altogether she looked rather remarkable.

She shook her head. 'I'm not sure, but I think fashion's somehow different. It doesn't really involve the feelings of other people so much, does it? Your family and friends would all have to be extremely level-headed and dispassionate if they weren't going to mind seeing you buried in a Campbell's Soup can. It's a bit of a joke.'

John was irritated by these comments. He was silent for a moment, disappointed. 'I thought we'd agreed that already, I don't know, I thought we'd talked about this and that you understood about how death wasn't a situation beyond irony, beyond a beauty of a different sort, beyond intellectualization. You sound very conventional all of a sudden.'

Melissa took a sip of wine, then looked into the glass because she could detect traces of sawdust on her tongue. 'I'm not being conventional, I'm not a very conventional sort of person. God knows. I wouldn't dress as I do if I was.'

John interrupted. 'That's just a part of your job though, isn't it?'

She shook her head, 'Well, no, I didn't have to work where I do. I chose to. Anyway, some people who work in fashion houses aren't all that bothered about fashion.'

John said, 'Fuck fashion. I don't give a shit about that. This coffin is something of great beauty and dignity. It parodies art and it parodies death . . .'

'In your opinion,' Melissa interrupted.

John was furious. 'Bugger my opinion, that's what it does. When it's completed it will be a thing of beauty in its own right. It will be something that pretends to be infinitely disposable – a tin can – but it will be something infinite, it will be the sum total of hours and hours of work and planning and precision and plain sweat.'

Melissa walked over to the wall on which the illustrations were tacked. She stared at them again and then looked at John. He was touching the handle of his metal plane, making a pattern with his finger in the dust. She could tell by his expression that she had offended him, and that confused her. She said, 'I didn't mean to be horrible about your work. It just seems strange to me. I've never been a big Warhol fan, maybe that's the difference between us.'

John didn't stop making the patterns. 'Neither have I, that's not the point. The point is something beyond Warhol, beyond art but about art. I can't be bothered explaining it again.'

She tried to smile. 'It'll be fun painting it, I bet.'

John said nothing. He was sulking, but not lightheartedly.

Melissa continued, 'I can see now why you thought the material was a good idea, all silvery and glossy. How will you line this thing?'

He shrugged, uninterested. 'I suppose with silver-topped wood tacks, all close together on both the top and the bottom.'

She laughed. 'I thought it would have to be sewn on or something. That was stupid.'

His silence confirmed her opinion. After a while he stopped what he was doing and stared at her. She looked such an inappropriate figure in his living room, brightly coloured and frivolous; she looked uncomfortable, and he wished she'd go. Eventually he said, 'Would you like some more wine?'

She didn't answer directly, just shook her head and said, 'Now you've built this thing it's not just an idea in your head, is it? It's more than that, it's also everything that everyone else may happen to think or decide. I suppose that the idea was something very pure but the object . . . I don't know.'

John sighed. 'I think that line of thought is a waste of time. It's pointless. I want to get on with my work now. You can stay and watch if you like but there'll be quite a bit of noise and dust.'

Melissa put down her glass on the mantelpiece and said, 'I'd better be going anyway, before it gets dark.'

John nodded.

When she had gone he felt very tired. He sat on his sofa with his legs drawn up and didn't move for several hours. Then he slept with his head resting on his arm.

Melissa sat on the tube feeling irritated and depressed. It wasn't just that she had upset John – an artist, a sculptor, someone who made things change, someone who was inspired – it was also that she couldn't make him understand what she meant. He had mistaken how she was, what she wanted to say, and had twisted it, had made it seem senseless. That wasn't what she'd wanted at all, not what she'd intended. In her heart she respected John for his determination and purposefulness, and she envied him. She even liked his ideas. But she wanted to see each situation from every angle, to uncover every mystery and to analyse it, to understand things completely. She wanted to be able to appreciate everything, the totality of things. She sat on the tube and thought, 'Maybe I only want total understanding because there is something wrong with me. Maybe it's like Steve says, that I think about things too hard, feel things as a kind of excuse for doing nothing. I wonder if that *is* what Steve says . . .' She couldn't clearly remember.

At work on Monday Steve questioned Melissa closely about her weekend. She seemed deflated, depleted. First thing in the morning he made her tea and said, 'You seem depressed again. Any particular reason?'

Melissa thanked him as she took the proffered mug. 'Yes . . . No. I saw John, you know, on Saturday. We had a bit of a row. I think I offended him, but in a way I think he was being a bit pig-headed and stupid.'

Steve frowned. 'How did it happen?'

She paused and looked down for a moment, unsure whether she wanted to discuss it with him. She felt very protective of John, possessive. Eventually she said, 'If you laugh I'll be furious. What he's doing isn't funny, it's just that I'm not sure if I think it's a good idea.'

Steve interrupted. 'Don't analyse in advance before you've even told me what this is all about. It doesn't mean anything to the uninitiated. Tell me.'

She sighed. 'Well, he's making this stupid coffin which is based on some stupid Warhol painting, the Campbell's soup can thing, you know.'

'Vaguely. You mean he's making a coffin which looks like one of the old Campbell's soup cans?'

He tried not to smile, but she saw his expression and said angrily, 'I knew I couldn't trust you. I knew you'd just try and trivialize this.'

Steve looked indignant. 'I'm not trivializing anything. I happen to think that it's an excellent idea, and funny – not funny-stupid – I mean a good idea.'

Melissa looked away sulkily. He sighed. 'For God's sake, Melissa, what's the big deal? Since when does it matter a jot what you think about his work? Your ideas are your business.'

She turned back to face him but couldn't think of how to reply. Eventually she said, 'I don't even know. Maybe I'm just jealous or something.'

Steve smiled incredulously, 'Of what, for fuck's sake?'

She shrugged, 'Of anything, everything. What do I know?'

He shook his head, amazed. 'Not of anything, Melissa, of nothing. You're not jealous of anything, it's just a stupid impulse that you've had, a pointless display that means nothing. Maybe you do have a reason, but I can't think what it is. Maybe you're just contrary by nature.'

Someone came into the shop and Steve walked over to help them. Melissa regretted having talked to him at all. She felt stupid.

John awoke early on Sunday morning. It was still dark outside. When he tried to move his body it felt weak and stiff. His mouth was dry and he felt as though his throat was sealed and his lungs were somehow deflated. He struggled to breathe. The atmosphere in the room was very dusty. After a great deal of concentration and self-persuasion he managed to drag himself from the sofa and on to the floor. His body felt as fluid as water, as devoid of energy. He thought, 'But water is very powerful and I am just one person, a single person whose body is no longer working.' He didn't even really understand what was wrong with it.

He dragged himself along the floor, into the hallway and slowly, inch by inch, upstairs. He crawled into his bedroom and on to the bed. By the time he was on the bed the sun had begun to rise. He felt too tired and lethargic to close his curtains, so closed his eyes instead and drew a sheet over his body and face. The colour inside his head was a red-orange; the colour of the light shining in through the skin, blood and veins of his eyelids.

He felt sad and resentful, languid. He tried not to think of Melissa but she was all he could think of. It was as though she had violated his great plan, his scheme, his purpose. She had made it into something without meaning, or rather, something too full of the wrong sort of meaning. At the back of his mind he knew that Melissa had merely been facetious and that what she'd said should hardly make any difference. He knew that a small display of conventional disapproval shouldn't be capable of affecting his purpose and his belief in what he was doing, that in many ways it should rather have reaffirmed the purity of his ambitions, the greatness and originality of his work.

At the back of his head was a sneaking awareness that his sudden depression and disillusionment were nothing to do with his work, his ambition, his aims. In actuality it was to do with the fact that he was dying, and his body was slowing down, perceptibly slowing down. He didn't want to think about it so he tried to think about other things as he lay on his bed almost too weak for comprehensive thought, but not quite.

He lay in bed for a full twenty-four hours and then got up, stumbled downstairs and had three glasses of water before recommencing work.

Melissa spent the following ten days debating whether to send John a card or a postcard saying sorry. In some ways though she thought it was best just to ignore what had happened on her previous visit and simply to visit again and pretend nothing had gone wrong, or maybe to start off by saying sorry. She decided that it was best to just let things cool off. She was relatively nonchalant and saw the scale of their relationship in terms of the infinite. She saw no reason why they shouldn't be good friends in the future if she gave things time.

Steve said nothing to her, but he was convinced that she was in love. In fact she was not in love at all, she was just bored and had nothing else to think about. A general sense of apathy gave specific things in her life more emphasis. Even so, she thought a lot, and often her thoughts were on John.

John carried on working. It was difficult because his body was no longer dutiful. Often it moved in ways which were of no use to his work at all. It had become a hindrance. But he made progress. After ten days he had completed his coffin's lid. The shape was perfect and he filed it so that it was as smooth as the flesh on his belly.

The following few days he spent in a state of half-wakefulness; sleeping on the sofa and only rising to open some tins of beans or spaghetti or soup which he ate cold, or to drink glasses of water. He listened to the radio for company.

Among the letters on his doormat was one from his mother, who was concerned because she had not heard from him and his telephone number was unobtainable. There was also a letter from his old girlfriend which said that she was thinking of coming home to England for good. Things hadn't worked out and she needed his advice. John read neither letter. Instead he dreamed of his silver spray can and his pot of varnish. He was nervous about doing the lettering because his hands were now so weak.

Eventually he felt strong enough to work again. He had a wash and opened a window for ventilation as it advised on the spray cans he was using. He worked slowly but with infinite care. When he looked at the coffin he felt so proud that a lump came into his throat. It was shaped perfectly in every detail. At either end the edges of the coffin jutted out slightly as they do in that place on tin cans where you fix the tin opener and squeeze. He had sanded a series of rings on the top and bottom of the coffin that radiated into a central circle like those on a real tin. He had even created a seam down the edges, a little exaggeration on one side, where his actual seam was. On the other side the join was virtually invisible. The tin was entirely coherent and faultless. To stop his coffin rolling about like a normal tin does when it is on its side, he had filed a very small part of the base of the coffin flat, but this was hardly visible and didn't really affect the tin's radius. He had also made four neat wooden triangles which acted on the same principle as door-stops. If he pressed two in firmly on each side of the coffin they supported it and curtailed any possibility of it rolling. (These he didn't spray silver.)

He coated the coffin a few times, and after a couple of layers of paint the essential woody feeling, a sensation of something porous and natural, disappeared completely. He wanted a very smooth finish so that the paint was reflective and glossy and shiny. After spraying the outside of the coffin he opened it up and sprayed the inside edges and parts of the inside so that the movement between the paint and the material would be as gradual and gentle as possible.

It felt as if he was building a house, and the temptation was great to try and put the material into the coffin before the painting was completed so that it would feel finished and snug straight away. But he resisted temptation and waited for the paint to dry thoroughly while planning and trying out a few letters and colours for the label in rough.

This was the hardest part. Things were made more difficult because he felt so ill all the time now, not just ill but inexpressibly uncomfortable and tired. He had begun to find it hard to take solid food and was also too exhausted to negotiate a trip to the shops.

Melissa's next visit was timely. By the time she arrived again he thought he was probably about to starve to death.

When he answered the door to her ring, after a perfunctory greeting he asked quickly, 'Would you mind doing me an enormous favour?' He told her the location of the nearest chemist (for painkillers) and the nearest shop (for soup), and handed her all the cash he could find, which he hoped would be sufficient.

Her arrival seemed like part of a continuous dream in his mind. She didn't seem real, she didn't correspond with his present reality. He had entirely forgotten about any disagreement that he may have had with her. He was more concerned about getting the job done.

Steve hadn't discussed John with Melissa again since their initial conversation. She had tried to cheer herself up and had acted as though nothing could be further from her thoughts. But she continued to think about him and worried about what it would be best to do. Eventually she decided that it would be appropriate to visit him. Two weeks had passed and she wanted to make amends.

She'd tried to phone him in advance on the off-chance that he had connected his telephone again, but he hadn't, so she'd decided to arrive on Sunday after lunch and had taken along a small fresh cream cake as a peace offering.

After she'd rung his bell she waited for several minutes before he answered. She didn't ring again or hesitate and turn away because she was sure he was in. The house seemed to fester, possessed and vitalized by the spirit within.

When John answered the door she tried to swallow back an impulse of sheer disgust. He looked like someone she had never met before; a stranger with a strange disease, a beggar on the streets of an alien city. His body looked broken and pathetic. As he greeted her he supported himself against the wall.

Before she could articulate her surprise he had asked her to go on a trip to the shops for him and to the chemist. He dug around in his pockets and handed her a small amount of money. She nodded, took the money and handed him the cake, for which he thanked her. As she walked away she thought, 'Presumably he hasn't remembered that this is Sunday and most shops won't be open.'

She headed back towards the Mile End Road where she'd noticed that a small newsagent's on the way to his house was open ten minutes or so before. The newsagent's had soup and painkillers in good supply. She bought six tins of soup and a couple of packets of painkillers, hoping this would be enough.

On returning to the house she knocked on the door instead of ringing the bell again and it pushed inwards under the pressure of her hand. He had left it on the latch. She paused for a moment then entered.

Initially she headed for the kitchen because the living-room door was pulled to and she knew that this room, his work-room, had a certain sacred quality to John. The kitchen was still dirty and chaotic, and John wasn't there. She called his name quietly but the house was silent and he didn't respond.

She put down her bag of shopping and walked back towards the living room. Knocking quietly on the door and pushing it open, she called his name again. No response. She looked around the room and saw him lying on the sofa, curled up like a cat or a child. The room was – if it was possible – even thicker with dust and wood chips than on her last visit. It reminded her of how the moon looked on TV, everything dead and silent, the air so thick as to make any movement possible only in slow motion.

She called John's name again but he was fast asleep. As she drew closer to him she saw that his hair and his beard were dotted with multi-coloured flashes of paint. His hands were mostly silver and white. His entire body seemed to have shrivelled but his hands now seemed incredibly disproportionate to his body. They were large and strong and rough like the hands of an old man.

After she had stared at John for several minutes Melissa turned away from him and towards the other main occupant of the room; the coffin.

It was in two pieces on the woodwork table. It was a gorgeous, glossy silver and had a white label with the beginnings of some lettering. It was perfect and intricate, very beautiful. It was impressive but also intimidating. She knew what power it had as an object, what (so far as she could see) it had done to John. It had worn him out and smothered him. She turned away from it with a superstitious shudder and headed towards the kitchen again.

Given that John was asleep, she decided that it would be a kind gesture to tidy up the kitchen, in order to make it a bit more habitable. She rolled up the sleeves of her yellow shirt, which was patched all over with bursting pink hearts, and turned on the taps in the sink.

As Melissa worked in the kitchen John slept on the couch and dreamed about his coffin, which was on a long conveyor belt heading towards an enormous oven filled with fire. Although he was a short distance away from the fire he felt it burn his face and blister the paintwork on his coffin. The coffin was initially moving fairly slowly on the conveyor belt but its speed increased with each second. He was trying to hold it back and away from the fire but it kept moving on and on, closer to the flames. As he clung on to its edges he shouted, 'You can't burn it yet, it's not finished and I'm not in it. I've got to get in it first. I don't want to go into the fire after it. I don't want to go into the fire without it.'

But the coffin moved towards the fire at a relentless speed and he could not stop it or climb in. Pulling at the lid he tried to tip the coffin from the conveyor belt, but it was as if it was stuck to the base with glue; his nails snapped and still it would not open. He jumped away from the coffin as it entered the flames and it felt as though he was falling and that he would fall for ever, as though he had jumped from a cliff and was falling, falling.

It took Melissa a good hour to neaten the kitchen superficially, but she was pleased with her work and full of a sense of self-satisfaction and piety. She really believed that she had now made a difference to the quality of John's life.

She made two cups of coffee – black because she had not thought to buy any milk – and took them back through to the living room with the cake. John remained fast asleep. She didn't know whether to wake him or not. His eyes were darting around under the skin of his eyelids as though he was a dog dreaming of rabbits. She smiled to herself and sipped her coffee. The house seemed very quiet even though the radio was playing at high volume. She helped herself to a slice of cake and ate it slowly and carefully. John seemed no closer to waking now than he had when she'd arrived back from the shops. His face was so thin, though, and his eyes ringed with grey.

She looked at her watch and decided that it was probably best to go. After finishing her coffee she searched around for a pencil and found a piece of paper that was blank on one side. On it she wrote: *Dear John, I didn't like to wake you when I got back from the shops. Your soup and tablets are in the kitchen. I did a bit of tidying, hope that's all right. Please phone me at work tomorrow.* She wrote the number in big, bold letters. *I'd like a proper chat with you. Love, Melissa.* She pinned the letter to the wall next to John's other diagrams and illustrations and then left the house as quietly as possible.

John awoke and staggered to the kitchen for a glass of water. He saw the painkillers on the side board and grabbed them, hurriedly placing several into his mouth at once and chewing them before swigging them down with a mouthful of water. He was indifferent to the unpleasant sour taste that they had left in his mouth.

Every sensation in his body and brain on wakening had been

immediate. Increasingly he was fuelled and energized only by desperate cravings and sheer necessity. He just had to keep his body moving, to satisfy it, to quell its pain. He could not think beyond these needs, these basic urges.

After swallowing the tablets he tried to open a can of soup but he did not have the strength to grip the tin opener and turn its handle at the same time. He also knew that when the strength in his body returned it would have to be conserved for more important work. Painting was now a priority over eating, completion was his only real desire. He slumped against the kitchen cabinets and slid slowly down on to the kitchen floor where he lay on his side and stared at the tiles, tracing each line, each square into infinite patterns and diagrams, into apartment blocks and fairgrounds and Meccano sets. The floor was very clean. He thought of Melissa for a moment before pain drove him back into a state like sleep.

Melissa keenly awaited John's telephone call the following day at work but he did not phone. Nor on Tuesday, nor on Wednesday. For some reason this lack of contact made her feel unbearably sad. She knew that her options were open to go and see him again, but felt that her welcome could not be guaranteed since he had made no effort to get into contact with her. She wondered if she had offended him in some way, or whether he still hadn't forgiven her for her frank behaviour on her previous visit.

Steve watched Melissa becoming increasingly depressed and listless as the week progressed. It didn't take much intelligence to guess why she was so down.

On Thursday he decided to broach the subject directly. She was folding up some T-shirts that a customer had unfolded a few minutes before. He was at the till putting in a new till roll. As he wound the paper up tightly and pressed it into the till he said, 'You haven't mentioned that guy John in a while, have you seen him?'

She turned from her task and stared at him. 'Why do you ask? Did he phone earlier while I was out getting lunch?'

Steve shook his head. 'Were you expecting to hear from him today?'

Melissa sighed and completed what she was doing. Then she straightened up and leaned against the shelves, tucking a stray piece of dark hair behind her ear. 'I don't think he's very well. Every time I go and see him he looks worse. I went on Sunday and he looked like an Auschwitz survivor.'

Steve pulled a rather cynical expression and her eyes widened. 'No, honestly, I'm not exaggerating. He looks all thin and he's growing this awful beard. He's really unkempt and the house is in a terrible state.'

Steve thought for a moment and then said, 'Have you spoken to him about it?'

She sighed. 'What am I supposed to say? "Hello, God you look awful?" I don't think he'd even pay any attention if I did. Last time I went to see him he sent me off to the shops to buy some soup and painkillers then when I got back he was fast asleep, really deeply asleep. He didn't look too good.'

Steve shrugged. 'Maybe he is unwell. I thought he was a diabetic or something. Did you wake him up?'

Melissa shook her head. 'I didn't like to. I hardly know him. I cleaned the place up a bit – it's really messy and dusty and dirty now – then I went home. But I left a note for him asking him to contact me here.'

'But he hasn't?'

'No, he hasn't.'

John had not seen Melissa's message because everything had been unfocused all week. It had taken several hours on Sunday night to drag himself into the living room from his position on the kitchen floor. He had almost lost all feeling in his feet but his hands were still clumsily movable which, he told himself, was all that really mattered. Standing was virtually impossible. Any fast movement was now entirely out of the question and everyday tasks like getting food and drink, washing or going to the toilet were now arduous and exhausting.

Using his initiative, he managed to rig up a bucket and washing bowl system in the living room so that he hardly had to move from that room any more. The bucket was full of drinking water and he used the bowl as a chamber pot. Most of his time was spent on the floor. He had pulled his coffin down off the bench and now lay across it as he painted it. After several attempts, he had managed to drag the central Warhol illustration from the wall, ripping it in the corners where the drawing pins stayed fixed into position. Melissa's note was now out of his range.

One of the windows in the room was still open for ventilation which meant that he felt very cold a lot of the time. But he saw the cold as a kind of blessing because it prevented him from sleeping and forced him to work, although his hand shook so much as he held the brush that he had to hold it still with his other shaking hand.

The radio was always on, day and night, and the tunes flew around the room like brightly coloured birds which he could not grasp, but he watched them and was dazzled by them. In all his pain he felt so happy and so righteous. He had never felt as happy before and he welcomed this feeling as if it were a stranger and shook its hand with great formality and offered it a cup of tea. But he only had water now, and after a few days the bucket was nearly empty and he had difficulty telling the bucket from the bowl until he sipped a mouthful of his own urine; but after a while his urine tasted only of water.

And so his time passed, everything in close-up, each letter, each colour, each movement of the brush the only thing, everything, his only concern. He had nothing else left to think about and that was tantamount to bliss.

Eventually he was numb to the hips and he smiled and pretended that he was a snail. It was nearly done.

Steve was really quite concerned about John and told Melissa that she should go and see him again, and soon, but she wouldn't go. She kept saying – and with increasing insistence and irritation – 'If he wanted to see me he'd contact me. I don't want to get involved and find that I'm out of my depth. He'll phone eventually, and if not, well, then not. The end.'

Steve kept saying, 'But what if he's ill and hasn't seen your note?' She didn't answer.

He also asked her about John's work. He felt an unaccountable concern for John and was interested in what he was doing; he respected it, he understood it. After their initial discussion about John on the Thursday he'd asked, 'How is his work progressing? How's the coffin? Is it nearly completed yet?'

Melissa shuddered. He smiled, 'A sensitive subject?'

She shook her head, 'I don't want to talk about it. I hate it. I think it's evil, I know it sounds stupid . . .'

Steve nodded, 'You're right. It does. It is.'

Seven days went by, uneventful days. Then a woman phoned the shop while Melissa was out getting lunch and asked for her in an uncertain voice. The shop was empty. Steve said, 'I'm afraid that she's not here at the moment. Can I take a message?' 'I'm John's mother. John is dead. I want to find out how it happened. I read her note on the wall.'

Her voice shook. Steve closed his eyes for a moment and then opened them again. He said, 'I'm so sorry. I don't know what to say. I'll tell her to call you back.'

She provided her number – it was John's old number – and said goodbye.

Steve waited for Melissa to return and felt sick at the idea of telling her. He served several people before she got back. She said, 'Sorry I've been so long, but I got distracted on Berwick Street. I found this lacy stuff in red and green which is really gorgeous.'

Steve smiled his response and then said, 'Melissa I've got a bit of news for you which I think you might find upsetting.'

She put down her bag at the back of the shop where they kept their private belongings, then returned to him. He said, 'John's mother rang and she said that he's dead.'

Melissa shrugged. 'I knew this would happen, I knew it. I really did.'

Steve felt angry. 'Of course you didn't fucking know. If you knew you could have done something.'

167

She was flushed and her eyes seemed very round. 'Don't you start trying to blame me for anything now Steve, that would be bloody typical. Don't make it look like I could have stopped this. I didn't do anything, so don't try and make me feel bad.'

Steve grabbed her hand, which felt dry, 'I'm not blaming you. Do you think I'm really as horrible as that? I'm just telling you what's happened, that's all.'

She took her hand away and closed her eyes. He said, 'Sit down for a minute.'

She shook her head. 'No, I'm fine, just surprised, well no, not really surprised, just . . . I don't know.'

Steve provided the word. 'Upset.'

She said, 'What did he die of?'

He shrugged. 'She left her phone number. I think she's hoping that you may be able to shed some light on the whole thing. I think she's a bit confused.'

Melissa suddenly looked unwell. 'I can't phone her.'

He laughed, amazed, 'Of course you must. He was your friend and now he's dead.'

She turned on him. 'Shut the fuck up, won't you? You're loving this. It's not as though you understand what's going on. You never even knew him. It's hardly your problem, is it?'

He smiled grimly at her. 'It's not my problem, no. It's his problem. He's dead. Maybe it's too much to expect you to phone his mother.' He felt ridiculous, felt as though he sounded like a stiff-shirted actor in a stage melodrama. She sat down on the chair by the till and covered her face with her hands.

Eventually an arrangement was made. Steve telephoned and they agreed to all meet up at John's house after work. Melissa said that she needed his moral support. He was her friend.

On the walk from the tube to John's house Melissa professed to be feeling rather sick. On a couple of occasions she retched dryly, bent double, clutching her stomach, but no liquid came from her throat, only painful, deceptive air. Steve tried to calm her down. He thought that this malady was induced by her nerves and he was right, but that didn't really help matters; it didn't make the pain in her belly and her throat go away.

John's mother answered the doorbell in a matter of seconds. She didn't look as old as they had expected, her hair was not completely grey, although she must have been in her early sixties. She was smartly dressed in a dusky-coloured woollen suit. She smiled thinly at them in greeting and beckoned them in.

Once inside, Steve looked around with great interest. He had imagined the house from Melissa's occasional descriptions and it was very much as he'd expected. John's mother was saying, 'When I got here the door was locked and no one answered my knocking, but I could hear the radio, and the curtains were open but the nets were still in place. I could just make out the shape of John on the floor inside. I got one of his next-door neighbours to climb in through the front window, which was open, and to unlock the front door to let me in. He took a while to get to the door – too busy checking the body, I suppose – and when he opened the door he said, "I think he's dead." He was dead. Afterwards I spoke to his GP and to another doctor that he had apparently been recommended to. He was ill, but in the end he died from something like exposure, a mixture of the cold and hunger and dehydration.'

She had explained all this as they walked to the kitchen where she switched on the kettle and rinsed out a teapot in the sink. Melissa asked, 'You mean that he had some sort of disease initially?'

She nodded, 'Something to do with . . .' – she frowned, confused – '. . . immune deficiency, I think. He was very ill, but it needn't have ended like it did. I thought that he may have told you.'

Melissa shook her head. 'I didn't know him well. I only came to see him here a few times, but on no occasion did he suggest that he might be unwell.' She paused for a moment. 'I was worried about him though. He lost a lot of weight over a fairly short period and he seemed to lose all interest in his appearance. He made out as though everything that was happening in his life was connected with his work.'

His mother shook her head. 'He resigned from work in the sales department about five or six weeks ago. He's been here alone since then.'

Melissa began to say something but Steve gave her a warning glance that quickly silenced her. He said, 'We both work in a shop that John came into, that's how we became acquainted.'

She didn't respond so he added, 'He bought some silver material from Melissa to use to line his . . .' He paused. '. . . To line the coffin he was making.'

John's mother nodded silently and carried on with what she was doing. She finished stirring the tea in the pot and got out some cups and saucers. Even though Melissa had spent a fair amount of time in John's kitchen on her last visit, cleaning up and filling the dish-washer, she had failed to detect what a large and beautiful collection of crockery John had accumulated. It surprised her. She was also confused about the various things that had been said about him, but she didn't want to say anything out of turn.

John's mother asked them how they took their tea, followed their specifications and handed them their cups. She said, 'I was hoping that you both might be able to explain that thing in the front room to me. I mentioned it to his old boss at the advertising agency but he didn't know anything about it.'

They entered the living room one after the other. Melissa still half expected it to be full of chips of wood and dust, she still half expected to see John curled up on the sofa, asleep. But he was dead and gone. His mother said, 'There was a post-mortem but apparently the body is still in a reasonable condition. Sometimes they have to cut away half the face, but they didn't have to do that with John.' She paused, for a second and then added, 'Thank God.'

They had all unintentionally stood in a formal sort of semi-circle around the coffin, each holding their tea in front of them as if they were at the opening of an exhibition at an art gallery, perusing the works on show.

The coffin had been put back together and was on the woodwork table. It seemed enormous and fantastical in this small front room, like a space ship, something inter-galactic. Steve smiled at it in wonder and couldn't resist saying, 'This is such a beautiful thing, absolutely incredible.'

John's mother clattered her teaspoon around in her saucer. After a short pause she said, 'Am I correct in assuming that this is a . . . that this is some kind of a coffin? I don't know what else to think.'

Melissa nodded at her. 'He's been making it over the past few weeks. Every time I came to see him it was all he talked about, all he could think of.'

She stared at it again, nervously. After a short silence Steve said, 'It's a real work of art, a real show of craftsmanship. Every detail is spot on. He hasn't quite finished the lettering, though.' He noticed a small bit of the material that John had asked for peeping out of the corner of the coffin. 'Is it lined yet? Did he manage that?'

Melissa turned on him. 'Steve, John's dead now. I don't think his mother wants to talk about this thing. It doesn't matter any more.' She felt angry at Steve, but the sharpness in her voice, like the top note on a penny whistle, was derived chiefly from her disappointment at finding out that John had deceived her in order to try and make her take him seriously. She got a sort of black gratification from finding out that her initial impressions of him had been accurate. She stared at the coffin with hatred and wanted to destroy it. John's mother was saying, 'Well, that is actually part of what I don't understand. I want to know what made John do this, it just doesn't make sense.'

Melissa answered gently, 'Maybe this project was just like a symptom of his illness. Maybe it was just a distraction.'

Suddenly her words were like weapons. She heard her voice speaking in this room, John's room, and it was as though she was listening to someone else, and this person was destroying all the things that John had said before, covering up his ideas and aspirations, burying them. John was dead now and what he thought no longer had any bearing. It didn't matter.

Steve turned to her, surprised. 'I don't think that's very accurate or fair, Melissa. John was always perfectly coherent whenever we . . . you met him. He obviously wanted to do this thing, to create this coffin. It was like a parting gift, an avowal of intention. It was obviously very important to him, given that in the end he sacrificed everything for it.'

As he finished speaking he turned to look at John's mother. Her face seemed puffy, as if she wanted to cry. She said, 'I can't pretend that I'm not bitter about this. There was a letter that I wrote him on the doormat when we got into the house, a whole pile of letters there that he never bothered opening. It's like he knowingly denied telling me that he was dying, like he gave all that he had left into making this thing and forgot about me. It would be untrue to pretend that I don't almost hate this coffin for that reason.'

Melissa nodded immediately. 'I think that it was a destructive and ugly idea in the first place. It trivializes everything, it pretends to be frivolous, but look what it did to John, how it cut short what little life he had left to live.'

John's mother was frowning as she listened to Melissa. She looked uncertain and worried. Steve saw this expression and felt compelled to interrupt. 'I think Melissa's wrong. John has created something very wonderful here, something that has lived on beyond him, that explains how he felt, that gave him purpose. I think that this coffin is almost like a gift to all those people that knew him and loved him in life . . .' He knew that he was essentially talking rubbish, but felt that it was suddenly necessary. 'That's why he must be buried in it; it must be completed and used.'

Melissa turned on him, aghast. 'You've got to be kidding! There's no way that this thing can be used now. After everything that's happened it would be obscene. This coffin is just a bundle of ideas, it shouldn't really have been constructed, let alone completed at such a cost.'

John's mother stood between them and stared at the coffin. She was unsure as to the relationship between the two of them. She wondered if they were a proper couple or if they were just friends. They were dressed in such strange clothes, in her eyes, that they seemed to slot into the same nightmare part of her consciousness as the coffin; somewhere modern and foreign and inexplicable. She wondered how much John had actually liked the girl. In the end she wanted only to do what was best for him.

Melissa was speaking again and she tried to listen to her. She said, 'When we first met John he was buying the material to line this thing. Even then, in retrospect, he was obviously unwell. He wanted to pretend that he was fine, but he wasn't. He said that he was building this coffin for someone else then, and I believed him. I think that was true.'

She knew now that this wasn't true, but didn't care.

Steve laughed. 'Of course that's not true! It's bloody obvious that John was building this for himself. He knew that he was dying and he wanted to leave his mark. It's perfectly laudable.'

Melissa frowned. 'I don't think that your artistic pretensions are appropriate here, Steve. This situation is more serious than that, more is at stake than a few silly ideas.'

Steve slammed his tea cup down on to the work-bench next to the coffin and a small portion of the tea spilled into the saucer and followed the base of the cup into a closed circle like a dyke. He saw this and thought, 'Eventually my lips will be the drawbridge.' Then he turned on Melissa. 'I can't believe that you're being so stubborn and thoughtless and insensitive. All that matters is that we do what John would have wanted, that we do what would have made him happy. This coffin is what he wanted, it's the thing that made him happy before he died.'

Melissa started to cry and shouted, 'But John's dead now, isn't he? Nothing can make any difference to that. He's done what he wanted and now it's time for other people to do what they want.'

John's mother looked at both of them and then said firmly, 'For God's sake stop arguing. I know what's best for John. What's best for John is that we remember him and respect what he's made; maybe that we even make use of it. I don't care if it's embarrassing, I don't care so long as it would have made him happy.'

Steve touched her arm gently and said, 'I'll finish the coffin for you if you like, and then you can make up your mind properly. I'll start now.'

He unzipped his tracksuit top, slung it on to the sofa and said to Melissa, 'Was he going to line the coffin on top and bottom using those silver tacks?'

The tacks were by the side of the coffin, glossy and ready for use. Melissa was still crying. She said, 'How the hell should I know? I don't want to stay here now, I want to go home.'

John's mother handed her a tissue and watched as she wiped her eyes. Then she said to Steve, 'Just do the best you can.'

Melissa was worried that her make-up had run, and went into the bathroom to blot her eyes. After a few minutes she returned and watched Steve in silence as he opened the coffin and unfolded the material to see how much there was. John's mother sat on the sofa and was staring past Steve and out of the window where the light shone in through the nets and glimmered on the coffin's lid.

Melissa thought, 'I'm going to do so much more with my life than this.' In her mind were a dozen plans. She debated setting up a clothes stall on Camden Market or going to work for Oxfam, 'To do some real good,' she thought.

After a few minutes she turned and left the room and then the house without saying anything else.

The silence in the room was interrupted only by the sounds of Steve working on the coffin, draping material and pushing in tacks. He debated how to mix the colours to complete John's work on the label. Under his hands the coffin felt like a crystal or a diamond, cold and complete, infinitely beautiful. As he worked, he couldn't stop smiling.

Country Matters

When Gerald walked out on her after seven years of marriage, Rosemary realized that she would have to acquaint herself with certain aspects of household management that hitherto had remained a complete mystery to her.

After three months she had conquered the damp above the tiles on the inside of the outside wall in the bathroom. She had also learned how to use the electronic meat knife. Her slices of chicken and beef were all perfectly proportioned and as thick as half of one of her fingernails, consistent in width, wonderful.

She had one friend, Emily, who worked as an estate agent in Finsbury Park. Often Emily worked evenings, showing potential clients around properties. Emily was also heavily involved with a pen-pal called Rolf who lived in Milton Keynes and sent her long, sweet letters, occasionally enclosing poems by Stevie Smith and Margaret Atwood. Rolf knew that Stevie Smith had lived in Palmers Green and that Emily lived in a nearby street. He imagined that Emily was a bit like Stevie Smith; creative, explosive, repressed. He liked the way she wrote her 'e's. Each letter was full of pzazz.

Rosemary cooked a lot of meat, seasoned it, sliced it, but Emily was usually busy in the evenings so she would set the table for one and open a small bottle of wine. Invariably she left the rest of the meat on a plate in the back garden, hoping to lure a fox on to the premises, or a badger. It never occurred to her to cook less. Part of her was still hoping that one night Gerald might return home, open the door with his key and declare that he had finally abandoned his new life with Claire from Accounts.

The meat was eaten, but not by a fox. It was consumed nightly by a tom cat whose behavioural problems had made him un-house-trainable. This cat Rosemary later came to call Rasputin, because he was a complex mixture of evil and confusion.

Initially Rasputin had belonged to an old man who was dirty and who had mistreated him, kicked him when he passed by and fed him on a whim. When the old man had died, Rasputin had been cast out into the world; a world whose gentleness and kindness were absolute in comparison to what he had sadly come to understand to be 'the norm'.

Rosemary had no particular attachment to the feline species. She liked animals in general but had never owned one because Gerald had suffered from a fur allergy which had been a perpetual cause of discomfort and asthma.

Rosemary had compensated for her lack by diverting all her affectionate energies into the large pool dedicated to keeping Gerald happy. Her favourite petting part of his body was the area of curly dark hair which descended from his belly button to his genital cluster. She padded this area like a fussy mother cat, pulling out tangles and combing it with her fingertips, stroking the hair into a glorious chestnut shine.

Gerald didn't mind. He always washed after sex with other women. He knew that his pubis smelled of lemon.

Four months after Gerald's departure Rosemary started attending a cookery class. She began to diversify in the culinary field. One evening she prepared a passable spaghetti, the next she created a particularly successful vegetarian stir-fry. She began to understand the joys of Cookery-for-One. There were no leftovers.

Rasputin (as yet unnamed) sniffed around in her back garden and located only an empty plate. He pushed the plate around with his nose for several minutes and then, throwing caution to the wind, attacked Rosemary's dustbin with the sort of savagery reserved in the feline species only for breeds of exotic large cat like the puma and the tiger. He became one hundred per cent primitive.

Rosemary was watching *Bergerac* when she heard a terrible combination of clattering and smashing, tearing and throaty howls from outside. She quickly made her way into her kitchen and switched on the strip light. It flashed several times as she walked to the window and then lit up fully and reflected its light on to her small back garden.

Her initial sighting of Rasputin by the bins was rather dramatic. The flashing of her strip light created the effect of a strobe at a disco, and Rasputin was the unfortunate epileptic stuck on the dancefloor in the throes of a fit. He had a large piece of tin foil snapped tight in his mouth – the foil had some smears of beef fat stuck to its silvery surface – and was rolling around on the concrete by the bins as though he was actually on the steep slope of a descending hill. He rolled (like a spinning top but sideways) from the bins to the far picket fence and then back from the fence to the bins. He was like a bubonic sausage, tumbling around in a frying pan, fizzing and crackling and ready to burst.

This display lasted for two or three minutes and then ended as suddenly as it had begun. Rasputin sat up straight, dropped the tin foil, licked his lips and then turned his head to peruse the scattered contents of the upturned dustbin.

He remained still and thoughtful for what seemed like an age. Rosemary was impressed by his deep cognitive reverie, his apparent contemplative serenity.

She liked him. He was thin and his face, neck and upper legs were covered in pinky sores. His coat was an intermittent ginger, and his eyes were half covered in their white sleep-sheaths. He was a bit like a mantra (she thought). When he was still and thoughtful there was something lulling and repetitive about him, something that pulsated calmness and tranquillity.

She went to the fridge and got out a bottle of milk which she poured into a breakfast bowl. She then opened a tin of spam and crushed it up with a fork on a plate. Every so often she peeked out of the window to make sure that he hadn't moved. Rasputin remained erect and immobile. Out of the corner of his eye he could see Rosemary moving about in her kitchen. The core of mad wilderness inside his scraggy chest fluttered and pulsated. He remained still, watching the light shimmering on the edges of his whiskers.

Rosemary opened her back door with infinite gentleness, bent down slowly and placed her bowl and her plate gingerly on the back step. She was sure the cat would run away.

Rasputin watched her and growled gently to himself. His throat vibrated like a guitar string. After a couple of seconds, before Rosemary had withdrawn – he didn't give a damn – he stood up, stretched, and then marched towards the backstep, Rosemary and the two plates. He wolfed down the spam and then (unlike most cats, who lap their milk with spiky tongues) he placed his face into the bowl of milk and sucked at the liquid with great force. He drank an inch or so (in depth) and then stared at Rosemary with a dripping visage. She smiled and offered him her hand to smell. He bit her hand and then dashed between her legs and into the house.

After washing her hand and dabbing it with TCP, Rosemary stealthily crept around the house, trying to locate Rasputin (by now he had been named), but he was nowhere to be found. The only indication of his presence was a large pool of smelly cat urine in the centre of her living-room carpet. Following ten or so minutes of fruitless searching she made herself a cup of tea and tried to concentrate on *Bergerac* again.

Rasputin sidled around the house like a blotchy marmalade shadow. He marked certain items of furniture with his own special cat scent, located in glands between and behind his whiskers. His tail was fluffed out like a stick of candy floss, his mood was predatory.

Eventually he returned to the living room. He sensed a tension in the air, he knew that Rosemary was ill-at-ease, uncertain as to his whereabouts, vulnerable. He tiptoed under the sofa where she sat and stared out at her two legs which looked to him like two pinkly fleshed chicken limbs; tempting, bitable.

Rosemary watched the concluding sequences of *Bergerac* and then, after yawning and gently touching and inspecting her still-throbbing bitten hand, stood up, picked up her tea cup and took several steps in the direction of the kitchen. Rasputin saw Rose-mary's lovely chicken legs move away, tensed his body and then sprang at them. He curled his midriff around her left leg with the aid of his front paws and pummelled the calf of this leg with his powerful back paws. He bit whatever flesh came to hand.

Rosemary was taken entirely by surprise. Her immediate impulse was to hit at the cat with the tea mug which she still held in her hand.

The mug cracked resolutely against Rasputin's skull and front teeth. She hit him three times before he released his grip and shot away in the direction of the hallway like a terrier down a rabbit hole.

Rosemary's legs were substantially cut and bloodied. She dropped the cup – as though it burned her hand – then ran into the kitchen and shut the door. She poured some water into the sink and used some damp kitchen towel to wipe down her leg. After seeing to her cuts and bites she dug around in the cupboard under the sink and located an old pair of Wellington boots which she pulled gently on to each leg. As she completed this task and considered her options the door-bell rang.

Emily was on her doorstep, tired after a long day at work and keen to get her feet up with a nice cup of tea. Rosemary opened the door four or five inches wide and peered out at her. Emily smiled. 'Can I come in?' Rosemary looked warily behind her and opened the door slightly wider. She said, 'I'm sorry Emily, but it's a bit difficult at the moment.'

Emily's eyes lit up. 'Is it Gerald?' She peered past Rosemary and into the hallway.

Rosemary shook her head. 'No, it's this cat I've got in the house. He's a bit wild. I think he might bite you if you come in.'

Emily frowned. 'Why on earth are you wearing your Wellingtons?'

Rosemary looked down self-consciously. 'Well, he just bit my legs, so I put these on so he couldn't bite me again. He's slightly maladjusted but I'm sure he'll settle down given time.'

Emily scowled and looked suitably petulant. 'So I can't come in for tea and a chat because you've got a wild cat rampaging about the house? For God's sake, Rosemary, get rid of it. You don't need this sort of responsibility at the moment. You're too vulnerable. It's silly.'

Rosemary bit her lip and looked uncomfortable. 'There's no need to say it, Emily, I know you're thinking that I've only let this cat into my home because I recently lost Gerald and I'm trying to fill the vacuum that he's left in my life, but it isn't like that. I didn't really invite him in, he sort of . . .'

Emily interrupted impatiently. 'I wasn't going to say that at all. In fact I was going to suggest that you took him to the vet's in the morning. If he's a stray he could have worms. Maybe you should have a TB jab if he's bitten you.'

As Emily spoke, a loud crashing commenced upstairs in the vicinity of Rosemary's bedroom. Rasputin had located Rosemary's dressing-table mirror, make-up and perfume. Rosemary smiled apologetically and said, 'I'm sorry Emily, I must go,' then closed the door and ran towards the sound.

The following morning – Rasputin had been locked in the hall cupboard for the night, but not without a fight – Rosemary spent several hours luring Rasputin into a strong cardboard box to take him to the vet's. She decided to wear her Wellingtons in case he escaped in the surgery, although she was sure that she must look rather foolish.

The vet stared uneasily at the howling cardboard box as Rosemary placed it on the surgery table. He said, 'What's in there, a banshee?'

Rosemary laughed. 'No, it's a cat. He's called Rasputin. I wanted you to look him over to make sure that he's in good health. I've kind of adopted him. He's a bit highly strung.'

The vet frowned when he caught sight of Rosemary's left hand as she used it to push a stray piece of hair behind one of her ears, 'He's scratched you to pieces.'

She nodded. 'He got my legs last night, that's why I'm wearing my wellies.'

The vet put on a pair of padded gloves and opened the box. Rosemary half expected Rasputin to burst out of the box like a streak of lightning, but he didn't. So she moved closer to the box and peered inside.

Rasputin was lying in the corner of the box, on his side, limp and frothing. His eyes were rolling about distractedly and his mouth was covered in foam. The vet stared at him for several seconds and then closed the box again. He shook his head and took off his gloves. 'I'm afraid that I'm going to have to put this animal down.'

Rosemary was devastated, 'He wasn't like this before, honestly.

He was fine up until now. He's just a bit erratic. I'm sure he'll be all right.'

The vet shook his head. 'He's obviously brain-damaged. He's dangerous. It's kinder to put him out of his misery.'

Rosemary put her arms around the box and picked it up. 'He hasn't got brain damage, he's just been mistreated and is a bit wild. I'm sure I can give him a good home.'

The vet smiled but didn't look happy. 'There's nothing you can do for this animal. I'm afraid that I'm going to have to insist that you give him to me. Keeping him alive is cruel. If you don't give him to me I'll be forced to report you to the RSPCA.'

Rosemary didn't put the box down; she took several steps backwards towards the door. 'I know he gets excitable, but . . .'

She thought of the previous evening when she had seen him sitting still in the garden, deep in his reverie, peaceful, benign. 'Sometimes he can be very gentle and peaceful. I've seen it. I'm sure that he'll be all right.'

She turned and left the surgery.

The following three days were nightmarish. Rasputin took over the upstairs landing and Rosemary's bedroom. He sprayed this territory with his cat scent and refused to allow Rosemary access to these two rooms. He had the advantage of height – which he used to the best of his ability – so that he could launch attacks on Rosemary from the top step of the stairs, thereby avoiding all intercourse with her Wellington boots. When he wanted feeding he sidled downstairs and mewed plaintively. At these times he seemed almost normal. Unfortunately, as soon as the food had been provided he became intensely tetchy and aggressive. Rosemary took to standing in the garden while he ate, fearing for his digestion and her skin. She bought him a cat litter but he proudly refused to interact with it. Instead he left sizeable deposits on the carpets and urinated like a giraffe.

On the second day a stranger knocked at Rosemary's door. She answered promptly, carefully peering up the stairway before venturing into the hall, and stared out at him through the crack in the door.

'Yes?'

He was tall and muscular and had big square teeth like a sheep or a goat. 'I've come to get the cat. RSPCA.'

He showed her his card. She slammed the door shut, ran into the kitchen and switched the radio on, ignoring the bell's ringing.

That night Emily phoned. She was brief: 'Has that cat gone yet, Rosemary?'

Rosemary felt paranoid. 'Why should he go? No one wants to understand him. I know he's difficult, but people have mistreated him. He can't speak to defend himself so I have to defend him.'

Emily sighed and hung-up.

On the morning of the third day Rosemary was standing by her rose bushes waiting for Rasputin to finish devouring his breakfast when the RSPCA man sprang into her back garden and pushed her up against the picket fence. She didn't immediately recognize him. He held on to her arm with one hand and took out his card. He said, 'Remember me? My name is Bill. I've come to get your cat.'

His hand on her arm was enormously powerful. She said, 'Go away. Leave us alone. I'm all he's got. He isn't doing anybody any harm.'

Bill stared down at her and smiled, 'How the hell do you know what he wants? Who gave you the right to decide anyway? You think you know what's for the best but you don't.'

He let go of her arm and strode into the kitchen. She ran after him. Rasputin was huddled in the corner by his food bowl. His eyes were hooded but he didn't growl. He was so thin. Bill bent down and picked him up. Rasputin didn't struggle. Rosemary was amazed. 'He's so calm with you. How do you do it?'

Bill smiled. 'He knows that I want to help him. Do you have a box?'

She moved towards him. 'Please leave him with me. I'm sure I can make him better.'

He stared at her in silence for a minute or so and then said, 'Are you very lonely?'

She clenched her fists, furious. 'Don't patronize me.'

He grinned, and his face was like the face of an extraordinary animal, a buffalo or a moose. He said, 'I'm going to kill this cat because it is the kindest thing to do.'

She wanted to cry. 'You don't understand . . .'

He put Rasputin down gently and then stood up straight again. He filled the kitchen. Something about him made her dizzy. An energy was in the room. Rasputin seemed very small and insignificant, like a mouse or a tiny kitten. Bill said, 'I do understand. I want to show you something.'

He put his hands to his waist and unbuckled his belt. Rosemary gasped. For a moment she thought he was going to hit her with the belt or expose himself. She watched his hands as he undid his buttons and then slid his trousers from his hips.

She could barely believe what she saw. His thighs and legs were completely covered in soft brown fur. He bent down and untied his shoes. He said, 'I have to adapt my shoes so that they look realistic, as though they are supporting a whole foot instead of just a hoof.'

He removed two large, round, yellowy hooves from his Argyll socks. They made a horsey clip-clopping noise on her tiled floor. She felt uncomfortable but couldn't resist saying, 'Do you mind if I feel your fur?'

He shook his head. 'Feel free.'

She stroked his fur back into place where it had been ruffled by his clothing. He smiled as she stroked him and then said, 'I bet you want to know the answer to two questions, but you are too afraid to ask.' He paused. 'Firstly, how was I produced, from a woman or a goat? Secondly, do I operate effectively in the sexual arena as a man?'

She smiled and blushed slightly. 'I must admit, I was wondering . . .'

He grinned. 'Well, I'm afraid we've got more pressing matters to discuss at the moment.'

He nodded towards Rasputin who was lying on his side near a puddle of urine. Rosemary picked up a cloth and ran it under the tap. She said, 'I'm going to clear this mess up and then I'm going to make us both something to eat and drink.'